THE BROKEN VOW:

VOL. I. OF THE CLANDESTINE EXPLOITS OF A WEREWOLF

BY

EVELYN KLEBERT

The Broken Vow:
Vol. I. of The Clandestine Exploits of a Werewolf
By Evelyn Klebert

A Cornerstone Book
Published by Cornerstone Book Publishers

First Cornerstone Edition – 2013
Second Cornerstone Edition – 2021
Third Cornerstone Edition – 2023
Fourth Cornerstone Edition – 2025

Cornerstone Book Publishers
Hot Springs Village, AR
www.cornerstonepublishers.com

ISBN 978-1-61342-133-8

Dedication

*For Robert and Jonathan Whose Ideas Open
Up New Worlds For Me*

Table of Contents

PROLOGUE

"What do you fear, my child?"

Granted, it wasn't the usual question of a priest in a confessional. But then again, he was no ordinary priest.

"Fear? Father?"

Her young voice quaked, sending a shiver of compassion through his heart. It was unfortunate to be so young and so afraid. There was plenty of time for fear when one became older and recognized the real demons of the world.

"Yes, my child, I can feel fear."

"I." There was hesitation in her young voice, and images of hardship, poverty, and even violence from her parents flooded his mind. It was ill-advised for him to use his powers in such a way, entirely too draining. But something about the young girl, no more than twelve, he thought, tugged at his heart — his old, well-seasoned heart. "I don't know, Father. I think I fear the demons that come out of the forest."

It became as clear as a crystallized picture in his mind that she lived in a province outside the city. The family had journeyed here for trading, and the rare occurrence, it seemed, to visit the cathedral for some religious reflection.

"Who told you demons come from the forest, my child?"

"My parents, my Brother — they said if I tarry too long and the night falls, demons and devil wolves will come and tear me asunder."

He bowed his head. He knew she expected him to tell her that was not true and that she was safe. But hers was a pure heart, and his, well, his was always touched by purity. "Heed your parents child and say your rosary to the Blessed Mother. And don't be afraid. Living in fear isn't a good thing. But be prudent."

"Yes, father," she murmured as he leaned back in the confessional box. Prayers might help her, indeed. Prayers might keep her safe from demons such as himself.

The year was 1350 in the town of Chartres, France, where I was, for a scant period of time, a priest. But only for a time. I had already been a werewolf for over half a millennium.

1.

THE SEER

It was stormy. The great dark clouds moved restlessly across the sky of the lakefront. And the water beneath shifted with an activity a few notches above its normal placid state. She sat on a stone bench, breathing deeply, trying to calm her mind and heart. Her very skin prickled in aggravation. She bowed her head and strove to still her mounting aggravation. She must, or else she would simply be too vulnerable. She would simply fall apart.

As she took a deep breath, willing herself to be covered in a white energy of protection, she sensed without even looking that time had run out. She was no longer alone.

ɓ

"Are you out of your mind?"

"Noel, you must calm yourself."

"Mother, you know I am knee-deep in planning my wedding. It's less than six months away. You couldn't possibly expect me to get involved with something of this nature now."

The slender dark-haired woman reflected little expression at her daughter's exasperation. "Why?" she said rather quietly. "Do you think Patrick would object?"

Noel frowned as mounting frustration threatened to take hold of her. "That's not fair, Mother. As you are very well aware, I haven't told Patrick anything concerning this aspect of our family lineage."

Noel noted a slight frown across her Mother's traditionally serene features as she casually stirred the cup of tea that Noel had prepared for her only moments earlier. Josephine Duverje had arrived unexpectedly on her apartment doorstep nearly half an hour earlier. As it was, Noel wasn't due for work until the afternoon, so she'd only anticipated a pleasant impromptu visit — certainly not the potential grenade now laid at her door. "Yes, my dear. And as I have said before, I'm not sure this is the proper approach. After all, I thought marriage meant sharing everything."

Noel swallowed on a dry throat and struggled to be calm. Lately, everywhere she looked was stress, stress, stress. "Patrick is different. I plan to bring him into things a little at a time. Besides, my involvement in this aspect of the family is limited these days."

"What a shame, you've always had such talents," her Mother commented fluidly. "Too bad you haven't taken more time to develop them. But whatever the case, my dear, you are part of this family, and with that comes responsibilities."

"I'm sure you could find someone else," she murmured resentfully, although she was already aware that this battle was lost.

And then Josephine looked up, giving Noel a bit of a chilling stare with her dark eyes that she remembered very well from childhood. "No, my child. It is to be you this time. So, clear away the clutter of this life you've arranged and prepare yourself."

ᴒᴃ

"Noel Duverje?"

She wasn't quick enough. She should have taken time to erect defenses to master her rampaging emotions. Her Mother must have known that she was in no way in the proper mental condition to deal with anything like this. "Am I mistaken?"

He was standing next to her lakeside bench — a man, not an old man, pretty youngish, she thought, but older than her. She forced herself to answer calmly, "No, you are not mistaken."

Then he smiled with a warmth that she could feel. He was charming, wonderful. "Your mother, I believe, arranged this meeting."

She nodded slowly. Yes, she had. Bless her obstinate heart. "She told me you requested help from our family."

Another smile and those eyes, wide blue grayish in shade but filled with light. He sat down right next to her in the empty space on the bench without as much as an invitation. "Yes, I did," he continued as if they were already well acquainted. "A bit of a historical connection that my family and yours possess enabled me to reach out for the aid that I rather desperately need."

"Historical connection?" she echoed, with perhaps too much disdain in her voice. It was a failure on her part not to be very amiable these days. "That sounds remarkably ambiguous, Mr.?" she pried directly. Again, it was abrupt and not terribly gracious. But on some level, she hoped to put him off enough that he would seek help elsewhere. All of this business was an irritant, interfering with her life. She turned her gaze back to the lake before them. The water had become more tumultuous, not unlike her mood.

"My name is Ethan, Ethan Garraint," he offered, evidently willing to ignore her rudeness.

She turned to him, again struck by his handsomeness, long ash-blond hair just at his shoulders. And a face, well that looked like it had been finely chiseled by some artist in stone — defined cheekbones, but again the eyes, a gaze that seemed to reach forward easily, pushing past her innate defensiveness, of course, not at all like Patrick with his dark, rough, brooding good looks. She sighed a bit, feeling an obscure dizziness sweep through her. "Well, Mr. Garraint, what exactly can I help you with?"

ᏨᎦ

"You remember the promise."

"Mother, yes, of course, but that was —"

The dark brown eyes hardened, "A long time ago." There was steel in her words that told Noel succinctly that this was an argument she would not win. "But that does not lessen the covenant forged between the survivors. Without aid from certain individuals, our line would have been completely wiped out with the rest of the Cathars in Southern France. So many of our ancestors were consigned to burn in flames, branded as heretics for our beliefs and our gifts. It was the first European genocide of a people. If not for the protection and generosity of a select few who gave us sanctuary, you and I would not be sitting here."

Noel, seated across from her Mother at the small kitchenette in her apartment, felt deflated, out of protest. Her Mother was still so connected to a long-ago past, one that Noel could scarcely comprehend. How could she make her understand that this was no longer her life? That she had worked hard to suppress the abilities that the Duverje bloodline had gifted her with. That she now envisioned a different kind of future, mainstreaming herself into a world that did not acknowledge the things that much of her family prized.

She bent her head a bit and sipped her tea. Perhaps, perhaps if she acquiesced this time, then that would be enough. After all, how often do such requests present themselves? Her eyes rose to meet her Mother, who was examining her speculatively. She wondered if she was reading her thoughts. There was no doubt that she was reading her emotions. At this, she was most adept. "All right, who do I need to contact?"

Josephine leaned back in the small espresso-colored chair. "Don't worry, ma petite. I'll arrange everything."

C3

He was dressed casually short-sleeved white shirt, and khaki pants. After all, it was already May in New Orleans, dreadfully hot weather. But he was looking at her strangely, as though her question about what exactly he wanted was a curious one. He smiled a bit, staring out at the lake. "Well, you do get down to business."

"Doesn't seem any point to wasting time."

She could feel distraction, as though his thoughts were being drawn elsewhere. "Well, in truth, it's a bit complicated."

Noel leaned back against the stone bench and closed her eyes. She didn't have time to waste here. There was too much demanding her attention now. And then she felt the unexpected pressure of his hand on hers. "Don't do that," he whispered.

She opened her eyes with surprise. "I'm sorry I thought you wanted—"

"Some things can't be rushed," he murmured softly but with a curious edge of steel in his voice.

She suddenly looked down, realizing that Ethan Garraint hadn't removed his hand from hers. Rather he'd focused his attention on the elegant, glistening engagement ring that Patrick had presented to her on the deck of the historic New Orleans paddleboat *The Natchez* only two months ago. Rather overcome by the awkwardness, she pulled her hand away from the contact. He looked up with an odd expression, a bit dazed, she thought. "Sorry," he said quietly. "You're engaged."

"Yes," she answered. This felt very peculiar in a way that the conversation didn't merit. "Look, Mr. Garraint—"

"Ethan," he interrupted.

"Look, Ethan," she began again. "I do intend to help you, but you must let me do things my way. Do you understand?"

"Yes, of course, I understand. But Noel, if I may, what you don't understand is the complexity of my situation."

She frowned a bit with increasing frustration. This seemed to incessantly be the way of it lately. She would pound her fists to try to bully events to her liking, and nothing, absolutely nothing, would capitulate and go her way. "Well, chances are I won't ever understand it if we don't get started."

And then he did the unthinkable. He laughed, laughed softly at her frustration. "Well, I see. In any case, our time together won't be boring." He stood up abruptly. "Since time is of the essence, I think I'd like to take you somewhere."

She stood up slowly in response. "Where?"

8

"No matter, I'll drive."

"No, I have my car. I'll follow you," she stammered a bit. After all, she'd grown up in New Orleans and most certainly didn't take rides from strangers, no matter how historically connected they were to her family.

And again, an elusive smile as though he found her amusing, "As you wish."

2.

THE QUEST

Life in Celibacy

Did I enjoy being a priest?

Not really, I enjoyed the company of women, and this was a drawback. Other than that aspect, the lifestyle wasn't too taxing, even in the Middle Ages. It was a haven of a sort. People eyed a priest with a special sort of reverence, infallibility, and exemption from suspicion. Not at all like modern times when everyone and everything is questioned, which for the safety of the general populace is not actually a bad idea.

Back then, however, the long dark robes hid much.

I was a werewolf.

And at that point in time, not the most civilized werewolf, definitely in a period of transition. Let us say I struggled with it, with so many things. But there were other secrets hidden in the order as well — a necromancer, a shapeshifter, a vampire, or so I suspected, and then of course there was me. And mind you, plenty of other fine gentlemen *who were just that, ordinary gentlemen. But also, some much worse than any of us damned creatures — those in mindless pursuit of power. Unfortunately, the Holy Church was a stomping and breeding ground for that sort as well.*

And I do wonder, in reflection at times, if they were much worse. After all, I was a monster, but not by choice, but they did choose it.

In those days, however, I was more concerned with controlling my nature and surviving than entertaining such profound philosophical concerns.

ᴄ൪

Noel Duverje was following behind him in a small red sedan. Ethan found her filled with contradictions, sensitive, delicate, aggressive, exuding frustrations — all of it a bit unstable for what he was entertaining. He supposed he could contact Josephine again and ask for a replacement if, indeed, this was the proper protocol in such situations. But he doubted it would do any good. Josephine Duverje did not seem to be a woman who would change her mind easily, if at all. For some reason beyond the obvious, she wanted her daughter involved in his "situation." And above all, what he needed now was a seer. Unstable or not, it was of the utmost importance.

He pulled his SUV into the driveway of the small house not far from the lakefront that he'd moved into just a few weeks earlier. He did so enjoy the proximity to the water. It was calming, helpful in clearing his turbulent mind. He waited in the driveway as she stepped out of her small, red, rather compact car. There were things he already knew about her, although he shouldn't. She was familiar, the texture of her soul, as though somewhere they'd crossed paths before, and she was bull-headed yet fragile — a terrible combination that lent itself to untenable disasters.

"What is this place?" she asked as she closed the distance between them.

He smiled with a smooth veneer that he'd cultivated for centuries. "This is my home, Noel."

ᙀ

It was a comfortable house, warm, airy, sunny, but it made her head spin, spin with dizziness. It was filled with vibrations, vibrations of his possessions, profound energies from the past. He was very old. She knew this, although he certainly didn't look it in appearance or attitude. He was relaxed, jovial, charming, not at all covered by the imprints of a dark and complicated life. And it really didn't make sense because of what she was feeling.

"Can I offer you something to drink?" he asked, momentarily shattering her impressions.

She shook her head with distraction, "No, no."

He paused in the middle of the large, sunny den now illuminated by the afternoon sun seeping through the skylights. He frowned, but a frown on him didn't look nearly as negative as it did on other people. "I interrupted?"

It bothered her. All of this was bothersome. It was clear that Ethan wanted to take things at a leisurely pace, and she, damn it, she didn't have the time. "Look, Mr. — "

"I thought we'd settled on Ethan."

"Right, Ethan, I don't know what you have in mind here, but I don't have time to take this meandering path you seem intent on following."

He was still smiling, but she felt something else now, a determination behind the pleasant blue-gray eyes. "Meandering? Yes, I can see that you're frustrated."

"I am willing to help, but we must get down to business."

He nodded. It seemed in acquiescence. There was a chair in the middle of his den — a heavy, large cherry wood rocker with a light beige cushion that he settled in, then gesturing to a nearby moss green sofa where Noel sat down. "I understand that you are pressed by other things, but this is a delicate situation. To be succinct, there is someone I need to find."

She waited, wondering where he was going with this. "And you want my help?"

"I need your help, Noel. I'm sure he's here in the city, somewhere, but disguised, cloaked if you will."

She felt again that peculiar wave of dizziness that seemed to accompany powerful old energies. "So, I need to find this person, and then what?"

He leaned back in his chair, no longer smiling, no longer much of any expression. "Then, I will kill him."

3.

THE WOLF

A Beginning

Perhaps, I should have started here.

Well, some backtracking, then.

So, this is how it's going to be, for now in any case. I am old, born somewhere in the year 400 AD, and then was reborn as an immortal — although admittedly, can any of us say we are truly immortal? All of us have a time, a mortality. I've never been one to delude myself. It seems a waste of mental energy. I can be killed, and don't think some haven't tried, made a sport out of it. Of course, they have. After all, isn't it great sport to hunt animals? And some would simply consider me an animal now. Yes, as I mentioned, a werewolf, a lycanthrope, or any more colorful name that might be invented for my particular predicament. At one point, I was known as Le Guerrier. I liked that one, but I digress.

This is my journal, my thoughts, my fallibilities. And some would say my indulgence, something I might say as well. I don't pretend to be more significant or important than I am. It's just that I've been around here on this earth much longer than most. I've witnessed much, and there are stories, oh yes, always stories to tell. I'm not sure if I will leave this journal behind when I am gone. Or if I'll burn it tomorrow. I've never been a terribly consistent fellow. But I have roamed, roamed this earth through many ages, and have seen the change in men. And have also seen how there is never much change in them.

03

She stared at him in disbelief. Had she heard him correctly? He wanted her to locate someone so he could kill him. "You can't be serious," she stammered. His eyes had never left her face, not changing expression, just calmly, intently focused on her.

"I'm sure, on the surface, this might seem a bit overwhelming for you. But I felt that if we were to work together, I should be candid."

She'd gotten to her feet, exactly when she couldn't be sure, but she took a step back from him. He seemed more threatening now, although nothing tangible at all had changed about him, just her perception perhaps. "I will not become an accomplice in some sort of murder."

He shook his head much too casually for this conversation. "It's hard to say whether it's actually a murder. He's not like you or me, for that matter."

Her head was pounding wildly. And his words were not connecting with her in any coherent way. "What are you talking about?"

"We've crossed paths many times before, and may I say not yielding pleasant ramifications." He'd moved across the room to her, but she'd barely acknowledged it. She felt so dizzy. There were images, powerful images flooding into her from his words — fire, scorching flames, and screaming everywhere.

It was horrible, the agony. She could feel it — the pain, the fear all around her. "An entire people practically just wiped out Noel," he whispered, grasping her arms. And then she felt something else in the contact, the cold fog of night wrapping around her and the powerful moon above. And then the devastating transformation was ripping through his body.

She shuddered in a sort of convulsion just before the blackness swirled —

ଔ

Ethan had felt the moment she began to collapse and scooped her up in his arms. He hadn't been fair, so abruptly throwing all of this on her. But he needed her help, and his senses, his primal senses that his particular condition imbued him with, told him quite acutely that time was of the essence.

He laid her on the couch, allowing her to sleep for a few moments. She was a delicate woman, tall and slender, with dark hair. Beautiful, he supposed in her own way, eyes large but shadowed, and oddly confused. He pulled a footstool up to her that he'd actually crafted himself. One of his many hobbies was furniture building which, for a time, he'd earned a modest income from not so many years ago. His gaze drifted across her sleeping form. There was an unstable quality to her, a perplexing one. His eyes wandered to the small, tasteful diamond glittering on her finger. And all he could sense around it was stress, confusion. It was a dangerous thing to be so gifted and not be of a calm mind. It left one vulnerable to all sorts of manipulations.

ଔ

She dreamed after the shade of darkness had fallen around her. It was a forest, an old one, perhaps ancient because the trees overhead felt as though they'd witnessed many ages of time. She was walking covered in a long shawl that she pulled tightly, protectively around her. It was cold, a mist everywhere that permeated the air with peril, danger licking on her very footsteps.

Chilled, she paused in confusion in the clearing just on the edge of the forest. Here she could see the moonlight shining quite clearly across a tranquil body of water. And then she felt the rustle in the trees behind her. She wondered distractedly if he would know her or simply kill her. She was terrified and yet mesmerized at the moment. She turned slowly, feeling her breathing literally stop.

It was the wolf, a dark grey wolf, large, powerful, muscular, beautiful in its way — meeting her with the palest blue eyes. She thought to scream, but she couldn't. She could only stand there frozen, transfixed, rooted to the spot.

Noel abruptly sat up on the couch, breathing deeply. Her heart was still hammering wildly from the dream.

She glanced around the room and saw Ethan standing near the mantle of the rustic stone fireplace, watching her. "You should go home and rest," he said quietly.

She brought her feet to the floor. "I saw something."

He nodded slowly, telling her quite succinctly that he already knew what she wanted to say. "Yes, later, Noel, let me walk you to your car." He crossed to her, helping her to her feet. And the contact, his hand on her arm, brought the image again to her mind — the unearthly wolf with the startlingly blue eyes. She was trembling, but she had to get out of here. It was too much, too much to take in.

CB

"You don't understand."

Her Mother moved smoothly across the small kitchen of her wood-frame house on Piety Street. "I think I do."

She fluidly put the small tea kettle on to boil on the nearly archaic-looking gas stove. "Would you stop for a moment and just listen to me?"

Josephine turned to her, her dark brown eyes registering little emotion. "Sit down, Noel, and calm yourself first."

Noel did as she was told, which had often been the case as she remembered in dealing with her Mother. She did feel anxious, panicked in fact, as though her heart were palpitating. Upon leaving Ethan Garraint's house, her first thought was to rush completely across New Orleans to her Mother and plead her case. And get herself the hell out of this mess.

"Breathe deep, focus on calm," Josephine coaxed from across the sunny little kitchen. This had been her childhood home. Her Father had died when she and her older two sisters were very young. Josephine had been a widow for over thirty years and moved into this shotgun house shortly after her Father died. It wasn't a large house, but for some reason, it was what her Mother wanted. Cozy when they were all there but completely manageable for one person when they had left. It had become clear to her long ago that this was how her Mother had planned her life — to, indeed, live the balance of it alone.

Noel closed her eyes and could still only see that moonlit lake on the edge of a forest. "I think there is something wrong with him," she murmured.

"Wrong?" her Mother repeated.

"Ethan Garraint, I think he might be mad."

Josephine settled across from her at the round, metal kitchen table. "Does he seem mad to you?" she asked.

Noel opened her eyes, staring into her Mother's face. Josephine was helping her, calming her. In fact, if she wasn't mistaken, she would swear she was sending her energy. "He asked me to find someone," then she hesitated. Somewhere it felt as though she was breaking a code, a confidence. But her Mother was adept at keeping secrets. Noel was more than assured it would travel no further. "He wants to kill this man."

Josephine's face registered almost no reaction. "He told you this?"

Noel nodded slowly, expecting something, expecting at the very least her Mother's assurance that this little endeavor was over, finished, but there was nothing. "I can understand why you would find that upsetting," she stated in a far too modulated tone.

"Upsetting Mother, it's criminal!" she responded hotly.

Josephine stood up, responding to the whistling of the teapot behind her. Without missing a beat, she took it off the stove and poured it into two cups she'd positioned on the counter. "You judge things by your modern perceptions, Noel."

"What does that mean? How else am I going to judge them?"

Again, Josephine settled across from her at the table, her dark eyes not meeting Noel's again. "Did he give you any details about this person he is looking for?" She felt a pain crop up in her chest. "Be calm," her Mother soothed.

"Details? None. We didn't quite get past the he wanted to kill him part."

"I see," she said slowly, "and what did you feel, Noel?"

Her Mother's dark eyes were on her again, and she did remember. "Fire, I felt fire and people in agony."

"Yes, of course," she said quietly. "That was from the other times. Our ancestors were murdered in the fires at Montségur. What else?"

"I saw, I saw a wolf, a gray wolf in a forest."

Josephine nodded, "Yes, he is very old, Ethan. And yes, he is the wolf."

Noel looked at her Mother with confusion. "What does that mean? He is the wolf?"

Her Mother serenely answered, "I suppose I should have told you initially. Ethan Garraint is a lycanthrope, a werewolf."

4.

THE GIRL

Ethan wandered the great expanse of his airy den and questioned his tactics, his methods, his logic, and yes, perhaps his sanity. Why he felt compelled to be so heavy-handed with his very young seer was a perplexing question to be pondered at best. He breathed deeply, actually catching the scent of the water from Lake Pontchartrain, although it was some blocks away from his home. He did like the water. It soothed the fevered blood that he could feel coursing through his veins. Yes, ever since he'd stepped foot in the Crescent City just about a month earlier, his blood had been agitated, and his skin crawled with an awareness that was at times maddening. That was how Ethan knew he was here. His very essence reacted negatively to his presence. And Noel, something about Noel made him want to shake her roughly out of her narrow perceptions. She'd needed a jolt, and he'd given it to her.

He sat in an overstuffed chair facing a large plate glass window in his house, light streaming in, warming the skin on his arms. He allowed his mind to drift, drift to a healing place, a comforting soul.

He breathed deeply and felt his consciousness drawn outward. Ethan had sensibilities, paranormal ones, but he did not consider himself particularly a psychic. But this soul, this particular unique one, was a special case.

Again, he breathed in deeply, but it was the essence of another place. He could feel light streaming in a room, a large room. And he could feel her delicate hands brushing across a book, a book of raised dots. "How are you today?" he murmured.

Her eyes, soft hazel-colored, were focused before her unseeing. She smiled, being accustomed to his intrusion. After all, he'd started this when she was quite young. "I'm reading Chaucer."

"Chaucer? That sounds cumbersome."

Another brilliant smile made his heart yearn for closer contact. "It's required reading. I'm in college now, you know."

Yes, time had shifted somehow. He never knew exactly at what point he was dropping in on her. "Ah, everything is changing quickly." He answered a little wistfully. After all, he couldn't expect everyone around him to stay the same, even if it seemed he did.

And the smile dimmed a bit. She was so perceptive. "What's the matter?"

He sighed heavily. Perhaps, this had been a mistake. It was selfishness on his part, and the more he visited her, the more frustrated he became. "Nothing really," not really true, nothing beneath a thousand somethings.

"No, I can see it. Red all over you, you're in danger."

He murmured, "Yes, I suppose I am."

"It's more complicated than you think," she said, staring outward as though her sightless eyes could actually focus on something.

"I am going to leave you now. I don't want this matter to touch you."

"Please be careful," she answered with deep concern in her voice.

"Of course I will. Be well." And then he came back to the present. It was a bit reckless. The last thing he wanted was for the other to learn of his vulnerabilities, exploit those he cared for. He stood up, still feeling her essence lingering with him. He couldn't help it. He hung onto it as long as he could.

Love

Some things come into your life regardless of how you feel about it — the rain, the storms, the re-shifting of the continents, and in my case, the return of a soulmate. I'd lost her so long ago and lived a life filled with incidentals, activity, just about anything to fill the void. And then I knew when she was returning, whether I wanted her to or not. And at times, I didn't. It complicated so many things. But I was powerless. It was a hard lesson to learn that I, indeed was powerless. This was fated. And so patiently and at times not, I waited for her.

 og

"She's panicked. I'm not sure she's the proper person to help you with this. Let me arrange —"

"No," he spoke into the cell phone succinctly and deliberately. He'd expected this, expected Noel to cry off, but there was something there. Nothing tangible yet, but he could feel it in his skin. She would lead him where he wanted to go.

"Be reasonable, Mr. Garraint. She's a child in all this. Noel's gifts are unformed, and she's had no interest in honing them. I had no idea that what you wanted would be so complicated."

He paced his back patio, a lovely little space with high fences and a small sculptured, brick-paved garden in the style of a New Orleans courtyard. "It isn't complicated. I'm simply looking for someone."

"So, you can kill him? That is what you told Noel."

He stared up at the sky. It was a clear, pure blue color overhead. And he thought about the night coming. The moon would be close to complete, but he could resist it if he wanted. Over time, he'd become strong enough not to have the transformation be a necessity. But that didn't mean that he didn't yearn for it, reconnecting with the earth. This city had strong energy bands that he could draw on to recharge his existence. But being so populated, it was complicated. "I'm sorry. I shouldn't have told her that."

"Is it true?" he could feel the concern in the woman's voice. Was it true? Would he kill this man he'd chased to the very edges of this New World?

"It's a possibility, Josephine. He's planning something, something that could be very destructive."

"How do you know that, Ethan?"

"Because it's in his nature."

5.

MONTSÉGUR

Memory

There are times that one would like to wipe away from the memory of the earth. But unfortunately, the earth holds an exact record of its history and ours. No matter how dearly men would like to rewrite it.

Long ago, before I was a priest, I was a soldier, a mercenary of sorts for hire, well before I became a better man.

In the early days, my early days as I am now, I embraced my fallen nature. I allowed myself out of grief, out of loss, and out of a willingness not to fight anymore to become one with my animal being. How I came to be this way is for another time. But how I lifted myself out of this baser existence has to do with a miracle and a calamity.

1241 AD - The Languedoc region in southern France.

The Albigensian Crusade was a dark moment in history that has been marked and, at times mismarked as a twenty-year military campaign initiated by Pope Innocent III to eliminate Catharism in Southern France. Its culmination was a pyre lit on the side of the mountain Montségur where two hundred five self-professed Perfects of the Cathar faith were unjustly burned alive for heresy and the refusal to renounce their beliefs.

Amongst the insidiously poisonous legacy of this particular crusade was the creation and the institutionalization of the Medieval Inquisition. But some time before this unthinkable, tragic resolution and somewhere after the beginning was when a man who so long ago called himself Etienne Gerrant first became entwined in the events that were to follow.

"Do you fear death?"

It wasn't a question that he often or perhaps ever considered.

Life in those days, at least for him and most others he suspected, wasn't much about cerebral speculations but instinctual survival. He'd spent years roaming the terrain of Medieval Europe — its countryside, villages, and cities often rubbing elbows with a profound level of poverty or, in contrast, a depraved excess of wealth often side by side and had kept himself largely untouched by either. He didn't take the time to question the justice of existence, nor cared to. He simply continued to live.

So, he sighed deeply, trying to acclimate himself to such questions that he couldn't help but consider a bit irrelevant and more than that intrusive. But as it was, this was required for anyone working for, having an alliance with, or just generally spending time around the people known as the Cathars. They insisted all within their general proximity spend time and converse with one of their Perfects or priests as would be a more apt designation.

The counseling session, as it might be termed in modern times, took place on one of the parapets at the castle at Montségur, deep in the heart of the Pyrenees. Upon reflection, the scenery was perhaps best described with words out of some fabled fiction. Accurately deemed as a castle, it rose high upon its plateau of limestone rock, peaking at about 4000 feet and being ostensibly formed by the intersection of the Olme Mountains, the Fau Mountains, the Saint-Barhelemy peaks, and the Soularac. The summit, which they were positioned near, offered a stunningly breathtaking view of all the surrounding countryside — unfortunately, a beauty at the time that he'd felt difficult to absorb given his particular state of mind. "Why don't you just move your people if you are in danger of being attacked?" he murmured. He was a soldier, yes, one for hire at the time who still planned and thought on the planes of pragmatic plateaus.

The man beside him, who granted he knew scarcely at all, looked at him with a bit of a frown. This Perfect was actually around the same physical age or rather the age at which he'd physically stopped aging, early thirties. But even in his current obtuseness, he had to admit there was a presence to him that spoke of one who'd absorbed knowledge well beyond his years.

His appointed tutor was dressed in simple clothes, work clothes as a villager or peasant might wear, not at all resembling what he recalled of the Catholic priests most often maintaining their adornments to distinguish themselves from the common folk. But then again, from what he'd absorbed in the short time he'd been in the region, the people shunned material riches, although they had accumulated quite enough to hire themselves a protective band of armed men, himself among the group. "We are discussing you, Etienne."

Etienne grumbled a bit, fingering the crossbow he had strapped with leather ties along his side. Talking about himself was usually a subject he worked prodigiously hard to dodge. "You are attached to the weapon?"

He nodded slowly with little acknowledgment while staring outward at the picturesque scenery before him with minimal appreciation. But then again, as was previously said at the time, he was a different man.

Ah, yes, the weapon. He hadn't thought about it much, but in truth, he was quite attached to it. He was a mercenary, a hired gun, if you will. And the crossbow had become a bit like another appendage, an aid to guard himself against the savagery of the world he now perceived. "It's been a friend," he answered.

Claude, for that, was the given name of this particular Perfect, tried to maintain the serene countenance of his particular station. "It is an instrument of death."

"An instrument that may preserve your precious skin one day Brother Claude," he commented dryly.

Claude had seated himself or rather perched near him on the short wall of the castle gazing outward over the mountainous region. "I once believed as you do, Etienne. My family was killed in a raid by traveling brigands, and then I was adopted by the believers. I never thought I would have peace, but I learned it, worked for it, and embraced their pure beliefs. I have no fear of death, so I attach myself to nothing on this earth. I recognize myself as spirit wrapped in a tenuous flesh."

He eyed Brother Claude a bit dubiously, doubting that what he proclaimed was even possible. It was more than true that from time to time, he had toyed with the idea of obtaining a release from living, even craving it at moments. But these were fleeting considerations, not of any concrete nature.

"And Brother Claude, is that completely true that this earth holds nothing of value for you?" Etienne prodded, largely because he doubted the sincerity of his proclamations.

It was an odd moment as he remembered, a quiet moment when Brother Claude slowly fixed his eyes on him — eyes of almost a pale green shade. And he recalled that he had felt the hair keenly on the back of his neck stand up in awareness or perhaps alarm. Of course, he had been a fool, a fool to disregard this moment. But as quickly as it came, it was gone, and that serene countenance retook hold of Brother Claude. "Salvation is an ongoing battle. First, you must believe you are worthy of it, my Brother," was his answer.

ᚷ

"There was silence on the other end of the line. And then she answered. "Ethan, you could be making a mistake. Noel is, well—"

"Unstable?" he filled in flatly.

There was a sharp intake of breath on the other end of the line. He shouldn't have been so blunt, but his mind was distracted by other considerations. "Well, I don't know if I'd go that far, but she is trying to sort out her life, and for the moment, I'd say she might have lost her way."

"No, I'm sorry, Josephine. I feel that this is the proper course to take. I feel—" and he hesitated, for that was the thrust of it. He had no reason at all to back this up. It was simply something he knew in his skin. "I feel that Noel will be able to lead me to Claude Barraud."

Immortality

Immortality is a curious thing. People dare I say, ordinary people — though many would beg to argue with me that anyone is

31

*really "ordinary" — don't recognize or perhaps a better word is ac-
knowledge the various creatures that inhabit the earth with them.*

*So, not to overlook those who live and die on a daily basis and
reincarnate on this earth; however, there is also an unfortunate bunch
of us, cursed or blessed according to your perspective, who live on
indefinitely. Or at least until some clever mortal finds a way to dispatch
us.*

*I am such a being whose life force is directly tied and strength-
ened by energy sources, points, or bands, if you will, across the planet.
I could allow myself to wither and die if I didn't make a concerted effort
to stay alive. Have no doubt at all that I have been tempted on occasion.*

*And then there are other ones, other immortals whose life force
is fed by other, shall we say, less innocuous methods.*

*Claude Barraud, Brother Claude, became such an immortal in a
roundabout, rather unorthodox manner.*

1243 AD

"How does one become a Perfect?"

"Do you wish to take the rites?" He was a youngish man,
perhaps middle twenties — Brother Guilleme, who he had
caught in the midst of tending to one of the many gardens in the
small Cathar village that had sprung up along the Northern face
of the plateau. It was a hot day, and the young man wiped the
sweat from his forehead but looked welcoming at his inquiry.
"Do you wish to aspire to the consolamentum?"

Brother Guilleme was an adept, not yet a Perfect. But he
had no doubt that he was well on his way to that goal. Everyone
in the Cathar community was addressed as either Brother or
Sister. In fact, even without any formal indoctrination outside of

Brother Claude's little counseling session, he had rather quickly achieved the status of Brother Etienne.

And oddly enough as well, during his time with the people, they even seemed quite accepting of his unexplained disappearances from the group during the full moon phases of the month. He would disappear for a week or so and return with no questions, just acceptance.

He found them to be a strange people, not at all like the general populace he had encountered across the country. On the surface, they were not so unusual, hard-working, although extremely well-educated. Every one of them knew reading and most writing as well — actually an unusual occurrence outside of the Languedoc region. In his travels, he'd run across more than one noble who did not have such skills. But foremost, they seemed at peace, despite the turbulent news from the North that an army was slowly sweeping the region, intent on wiping out anyone even loosely connected with their way of life.

No, they weren't by any means sheep waiting for the slaughter. Not unlike him, more and more military defenders were being gathered in the village of Montségur in anticipation of a coming siege. But outside of this, there was still the hope that the threat from the North would dissipate. It was alien to his nature this kind of faith. But he had to admit it was catching. Just living amongst them had lulled him to a degree into an odd sort of tranquility that all of his brittle edges couldn't seem to resist.

"So, what exactly is this consolamentum?"

Guilleme smiled, dusting off a sort of well-worn floppy hat that had been lying near him on the ground. "It is the transformation, the spiritual baptism, that aligns you with your spirit. Anyone becoming a Perfect or getting ready to leave this world goes through the spiritual baptism."

He nodded, not really understanding at all. "Sounds quite mystical."

He looked at him a bit oddly as though trying to evaluate his intent, which in retrospect, would have been impossible since he had none. His questions were born of nothing personal, nothing sinister, just aimless curiosity. "It is completely binding."

"Binding?" he questioned.

"There are vows taken, serious vows that if one breaks could be catastrophic to the soul."

Mysticism, he was not unacquainted with it nor its unyielding consequences. Quite pointedly, forces of darker esoterism were responsible for his present state. So, when Brother Guilleme told him that there were consequences to breaking the vows of the consolamentum, he tended to believe him and tended to want to keep his distance from it.

As a young man, he had held ideals, boundaries of right and wrong, good and evil if you will, then calamity and extraordinary revelation that perhaps all human souls were better off not experiencing had twisted his perception and blurred those boundaries forever. In short, he could never guarantee that he would not break a vow, so it was best in his fallible code just not to take them. Of course, the vow never to take a vow was one he broke eventually as well, not so very unexpected upon reflection.

6.

SELF-AWARE

"Are you all right?"

Noel sat up in her bed, awoken from a dream state by her cell phone. Her head was still spinning, trying to achieve some sort of orientation. "Noel," the voice repeated, or was it her dream calling? Had she answered? Had she spoken at all?

"Noel."

"Yes, I'm all right."

"I called the museum. They said you weren't coming in today." Her head was throbbing. That was right. She'd called them earlier after her visit with her mother. Noel was the Exhibitions Coordinator at the New Orleans Museum of Art — a somewhat fluid position that allowed her to pursue her doctoral degree at Tulane University in Classical Studies.

"I wasn't feeling well. Sorry, Patrick."

There was silence. Vaguely she wondered if it was disapproval. Patrick was a bit of a dichotomy, supportive but also pragmatic. Supportive of her job at the museum, less about her chosen field of study. *"It isn't a practical choice. You have to think about the future, about laying a foundation for our future."* Patrick was a lawyer, a cooperate lawyer, all about laying foundations and being realistic in this doggy dog world. Sometimes she loved that about him feeling the need for groundedness in her life, security, but other times— "Do you need to see a doctor?"

"No, just rest, I think."

"I'll stop by after work." She glanced at the clock. It was after three. He'd be by around six.

"Okay," she murmured.

"I'll bring some Chinese."

"Yeah, okay," again.

"You're sure you're all right." He was concerned. That she needed, that she could hang onto even if there were no way in the world she could share what was happening.

"Yes, fine, sounds good," and then he hung up. He didn't say he loved her. In fact, he rarely said it. And she told herself that this made it much more meaningful when he did.

1243 AD

"Minds aren't separated, or rather they don't have to be."

Sister Bruna, a Perfecta who he was told had recently received the consolamentum spoke to him quietly with a soft voice that he remembered well. She was married to another one of the military personnel, who had also opted to take the rite, an occurrence which was not unusual, particularly closer to the final days. "Why don't you take your family and leave here?" He was concerned about the families here. The Cathars, which consisted of the Perfecti and the Credenti, or believers who had not taken the final rite, were not violent people willing to take up arms. But there were soldiers brought in as defenders that numbered over a hundred who also came with their families now housed behind the fortress walls of Montségur.

She looked at me as though my words were senseless. "This is our home now, our faith. There is more at stake than personal consideration. Surely, you can understand that, Etienne."

Of course, he didn't understand though he wanted to. He had spent literally several hundred years looking out for his own hide with no grander consideration than that. At that moment, the idea of a greater purpose tended to elude him. "Sister Bruna, you know that their numbers are too great. The church is rallying against you all. You could hide, start again somewhere else." He hadn't intended to be so candid, but there seemed no help for it.

Again, she looked at him with eyes that he could still remember, soft, serene — intent, it seemed on penetrating that hard shell he had spent so much time cultivating. "Some will. We won't be lost, Etienne. But the change is coming, and we are prepared for it. You can't attach yourself to the things of this Earth, or it will chain you. Our kingdom is elsewhere, as is yours."

He shook his head, staring blindly ahead, torn by a mounting concern for these good people and, somewhat against his will, a growing desire to embrace their philosophy. "You don't understand, Sister. The Earth is what keeps me alive." He stumbled upon those last words.

But she continued to eye him with a measure of compassion that, at the time, he felt keenly that he didn't deserve. "I see you believe that. Then our Lord must have more work for you here."

"And you?" he murmured.

Softly she spoke, "I can already hear the call home."

37

Awareness

"Minds aren't separated, or rather they don't have to be." This was the beginning of my training in the psychic realm. The priest and priestesses of Montségur taught me the complexities and simplicities of meditation, of temporarily dispatching the physical and diving into the well-spring of a universal energy that connects us all. Utilizing their training, I could feel and hear the clamor of others' thoughts, feelings, desires, unless, of course, they were deliberately blocked. And most people aren't self-aware enough to do such a thing, not conscious enough about themselves.

There comes a time in every lifetime if one becomes even remotely self-aware where you have to question and ponder your purpose in this world.

More succinctly, why am I here?

I think perhaps for some, they might escape blissfully through their time on Earth being untouched by such weighty concerns. It's hard to say whether I envy or pity such an existence.

But granted, some of us do come to this plateau sooner and others later.

For me, it was later, but then again, I've never claimed to have lived anything remotely resembling a normal lifetime.

☙

Noel slept but not a restful sleep. There was too much cascading through her troubled mind. Her mother had always told her and her two sisters that they were special, different, and when they found someone to share their life with, it would be someone who could accept fully and appreciate who they were.

Lilah, the oldest, had married a doctor who'd become a holistic healer at the Edgar Cayce Center in Virginia Beach. Genevieve was living overseas in France with her husband, who was a professor of Anthropology at a University in Lyon. And Noel was getting ready to marry a cooperate lawyer.

"Noel, are you quite sure? He seems, well —"

"Did you want to say normal?"

Lilah wrinkled her nose a bit, as she was apt to do when she was displeased. Noel remembered it from childhood. It was a little tic she'd adopted once it dawned on her that she couldn't push her little sister around anymore. "No, I was going to say different, different from you."

She hesitated, letting her defenses down ever so slightly. "That's what I like about him, Lilah. He suits me."

It was Christmas, this past Christmas, when Patrick had proposed, and she'd announced the news to the visiting family. Then, of course, later in the evening, when most had gone home or gone to bed, Lilah had cornered her in her mother's small kitchen. Lilah was well into her thirties, her dark hair pulled tightly into a bun and her hazel-colored eyes fixing on Noel speculatively. "You've been very unhappy, haven't you, Noel?"

It hit her badly, a bit like a heavy rock pitched right at her stomach. It truly wasn't as if her sister meant to undermine her, but not meaning to didn't mean that it wasn't accomplished all the same. "Where is that coming from?"

She shook her head slowly. "I don't know. I just feel it from you, sadness, loneliness. Are you sure that this fellow isn't just some sort of a band-aid that came along?"

Now she was pissed off. She was well aware of her sister's empathetic inclinations but calling her fiancé a band-aid. "You do realize how out of line you are here?"

She grimaced, "I'm just worried about you."

"That is no excuse for saying such insulting things."

And then Noel had moved to leave the room. "Are you going to tell him about the family?"

She spun around, feeling the rage ripping through her veins. "That is none of your business."

And then she headed toward the doorway, just hearing her sister's last comment. "By the way, happy birthday Noel."

It was true. Noel was a Christmas baby, hence the name Noel. It had made her different, as if she really needed a reason to be any more different in the world. But she pushed away unpleasant recollections and allowed herself to be drawn into sleep, but not an untroubled one.

7.

The Consolamentum

March 1244 AD

"You must take it, Brother."

"It is impossible." A whole room of them in the castle that now had been laid siege to for nearly a year, a siege that had been withstood until the betrayal. The incomprehensible betrayal of Brother Claude who had abandoned the community only to serve as a guide for the Basque mercenaries hired by the church, leading them along the secret paths and enabling them to massacre the guards along the eastern barbican of the castle.

"It is essential. Brother Etienne, we need you to help in the escape."

"There's still time to make a complete surrender. You can agree to their terms, recant—"

"Our faith, Brother?" It was young Brother Arnaud, so recently a Perfect. In fact, the whole room of them were Perfects, all having taken the consolamentum. Many soldiers had fully converted, willing to face their impending execution at the hands of the so-called true believers. That was the power of the truth of their faith, the power of these people. All had embraced this, all except him.

He put his hand on Arnaud's shoulder. He didn't want to understand. He had fought against it as long as he could, yet painfully, he did. Arnaud was so young, his full pure life ahead of him, but he was willing to lay it down. "To live, Arnaud."

"I will live, Brother, but not in this world. In my father's world."

It pierced his heart, the wisdom in that young face. How long had he lived on this earth yet never had achieved such devotion to anything? "We need you, Brother, to lead the escape, to protect our sacred documents, and bring them to a safe haven. But to do so, you must fully enter into our Brotherhood."

His throat was dry with grief, dry and parched from the knowledge of what was to come. "Brother Claude entered into it but then betrayed you. How do you know I won't break my vows as well?"

They continued as though they simply disregarded his fears. "You must hide for a time, Etienne. It won't be safe. Once you put our treasure into safekeeping, head to the village of Chartres and contact Monsignor Raseire. He is a sympathizer and will help protect you."

It was overwhelming — the pressure he felt, the agony of what was coming. He'd never felt so literally torn apart in his life, and he'd lived for such a long time. But the enormity of what was happening, what they were asking, was almost more than he could bear.

"You want me to go find refuge with the devils that are destroying you?"

He was an older man, Brother Guidrade, a much older man than the others, who spoke to him calmly, "Yes, Etienne, I know you. I know you believe you are cursed. But I believe there is work for you on this earth, and the burden that you carry will transform you. Don't be afraid to take the initiation. It will give you strength and eclipse any other vows you take and are forced to break during your tenure on this earth."

How dare they, he thought, as he battled himself. How dare they drag him up from the cesspool of oblivion to which he'd consigned his life and make him feel again, restore his humanity. How dare they and now ask this of him? His heart was literally breaking for these good people, for himself, for his inability to do anything to stop what was coming. How could the world be so unjust? How could their God allow this to happen? But then they told him often that their God was not of this world.

Brother Guidrade rested his hand on his shoulder, and he felt the warm heat of pure energy pass into him. He knew he would do as they asked. He did not have the strength to resist, to combat the sheer purity of their faith. And one day, he vowed, as binding as any vow he would ever take, he would find their betrayer and bring him to his knees.

ༀ

The sky overhead rumbled with a stormy intent as darkness began to fall. She shivered, although she was fully conscious of her dream state. She ascended an uncertain path with bare feet scraped by stone and rock. It was a curious path, not well trodden, twisting, and sometimes almost entirely impeded by dirt and rock debris. But she continued the ascent for some time even as it disappeared into the side of the tall wall, barely discernable now in the shadows. But she entered somewhere within, or rather beneath the structure, where the path had transformed into a small tunnel — damp, moldy smelling, where she was forced to crouch. At times, the walls scraped along her shoulders, but she continued forward. For she knew to stop was death, a cold, suffocating, torturous death. This she knew with no one telling her because she knew dreams. She'd studied them with her grandmother. There are rules to dreams, and you must always learn them.

Noel did not panic. She just continued to feel the rules, to push forward, forward even as the rocky ground bit painfully at her bare feet, push forward even as breathing became so difficult. At times, she shut her eyes, grasping blindly at the slimy stone walls, but eventually, she saw a light, a light leading outside. And mercifully, she stepped into the cool night just as the rain began to beat down on her face. She stood on some sort of ledge, and her eyes could barely make out the ancient stone structure now — walls and curved turrets, so old.

There was a light, but it was within, within an open archway that she dragged herself through. It was so quiet here as she discovered a chamber, a large chamber with an ornamental stone floor. Torches placed on the walls illuminated the interior as she moved further inside.

Her feet ached, stabbed with pain, but she wouldn't look down at them. She knew they were bleeding, and the light cotton gown that she wore, no more than a white shift, was drenched from the rain. With effort, she dragged herself to the center, a polished, gleaming, mosaic-looking floor designed intricately with various interlocking geometric shapes. It almost glowed beneath the reflection of the firelight — beautiful colors, blues and greens, and bold slashes of red. But her feet bled as she inched painfully across the gleaming floor. And she shivered from the cold, a chill that no warmth could seem to touch.

It was some moments that she stood in the center, in confusion as to why she was here before she realized that she was not alone. Her attention was drawn to the inner doorway. It was enclosed in shadows, but barely perceptible was a figure that stood silently as though awaiting her acknowledgment. But she could not speak. So, in time, of their own accord, the shadows shifted and moved towards her, mutating into the form of a man dressed in robes, a long black hooded cloak. "I'm sorry, Noel, about the journey, but you had to travel this way in order to reach me." The voice was low, and the texture smooth as though it could easily melt back into the darkness.

"Who?" She whispered because that was all she could manage to get out in her present state.

Very quietly and fluidly, he pulled back the hood, revealing an ashen, gaunt face, pale with coal-black hair and eyes of a light green shade. "You traveled through the secret tunnel, the one, the attackers used to gain their victory over the Cathar people. The one I gave them access to." Her head spun, telling her clearly now that the dream was ending. "I have a message for you, Noel. Tell Brother Etienne that his quest is folly. To continue to pursue me will take a higher toll than he is willing to pay. Remember this, Noel."

Then he reached out with his hand. His flesh was like ice as he put his palm directly on her forehead, but then it burned, singeing like fire.

C03

She woke, sitting up in her bed. The front doorbell was ringing, but for endless moments, she simply sat frozen, trembling from terror.

Finally, she forced herself up on shaking limbs, not even checking her appearance in the mirror before she headed to the front door. She had no concept of the time or much of anything, just the strange burning sensation she felt on her forehead, still hurting like a phantom left over from the dream. Noel didn't bother to check who it was before she opened the door. It was Patrick. She knew his essence.

A strange expression flickered across his face when they first made eye contact, his dark eyes registering a bit of surprise. "You do look ill, Noel. Maybe you should see a doctor." He commented with a measure of alarm as he crossed the threshold.

She shook her head, closing the door behind him, then folding herself into his arms for a crushing hug that she instigated and needed desperately. She needed his stability. She needed to keep grounded in his world. That was the only release from the growing pressure inside her.

8.

REACHING INTO THE PAST

"And that was all he said?"

Ethan watched her as she nervously crossed the floor of his den. It had been quite early and unexpected that she'd arrived on his doorstep. Just after seven, with no advanced notice, and to compound this, there were several things that struck him as alarming. It was only yesterday that he'd first met Noel Duverje out at the lakefront, but already he sensed a marked deterioration in her, an unraveling, if you will. "Why don't you sit down, Noel? I can get you some coffee," he commented smoothly.

She shook her head, almost frenzied. "No, I'm only telling you this for your sake. It was clearly a warning."

He had been observing her carefully since she arrived, but now he closed his eyes, trying to pinpoint what was occurring with her. In his time with the Cathars, he had learned some meditation techniques as well as the ability to tap into psychic abilities that they claimed all beings possess, albeit to different degrees. In bits and pieces, he could see the contact she'd made with Claude and the energy he'd pulled from her. Clearly, that accounted for the deterioration and, dare he say, instability. "I didn't expect him to contact you directly," he said quietly.

She stopped her pacing at least momentarily and faced him. "Yes, why would he do that? He seems very powerful and confident. I'm not even sure where we were."

The vision emerged clearly within his mind. "Montségur, no doubt, and yes, he may be powerful though perhaps not as powerful as he'd like us to think. And again, why would he contact you?" he murmured almost to himself. "That is a good question."

Her eyes widened in fear. "I want out of this."

Softly he replied, "It might be a bit late for that, Noel."

"I don't know how I can help you."

"Well, if he can find you, perhaps you can help me find him." She was pale, and he could feel just with his normal senses that her blood pressure was up. "Please sit down, Noel," he said a bit more sternly than perhaps he should have.

But finally, she listened and sunk down onto the dark green sofa across from his chair. "Is he like you?" she asked shakily.

"Like me?"

"My mother told me that you were —" and she hesitated. "It sounds so odd to say, a werewolf."

He couldn't quite smother a smile. It seemed so hard for her to get the words out. "No, he's not like me. But he is an immortal of sorts."

"So, you know what he looks like. It shouldn't be so hard to find him."

And then the smile faded. "No, actually, Noel, that's just the thing. What you saw in your dream was what Claude Barraud looked like in the 13th century. Now, well, he could look like anyone."

1244 AD

It is a difficult thing to wrap one's understanding around the idea of cause and effect rather than sin and punishment. But in his time at Montségur, he did manage to soak up this concept and, at the eleventh hour, finally did agree to take the initiation of the consolamentum.

It was a rite reserved for those aspiring to be Perfects or Perfectas and for those on the edge of leaving this world near death — a sort of last rite, as modern people would interpret it.

But being who he was and even more so than that, for all that he had done, he was afraid. In truth, he did not consider himself worthy in any respect.

"Brother Etienne, you have a long life ahead of you on this earth before you leave it. You will gain strength through this initiation." Brother Guidrade had tried to explain in earnest, although this reassurance did little to quell his fears.

They were in a chamber, hidden deep within the castle, reserved specifically for such sacred ceremonies and initiations. Around him, ten or so Perfects had gathered late in the night for this very purpose. All of them were deeply exhausted. It had become clear that Brother Claude's betrayal had gone beyond leading the Basque mercenaries to the vulnerable barbican but also tampering with the only water supply within the fortress. Dead birds and rats had been found in the cistern, contaminating it thoroughly. It was painfully apparent to all that this went beyond mere coincidence. It was another link to a much larger plan. With water, the Cathars could have survived indefinitely, but without it, their defeat was inevitable. "You don't understand," he struggled to explain, "I have not lived a holy life. There is much blood on my hands."

It was true that he had lived for some time without thought of consequence. This, indeed, was one particular side effect of immortality. It made you callous, not respectful of your time on earth. After all, what he had in great supply was time and quite understandably had not expected to be answerable for how it was spent.

But Brother Guidrade was undaunted. "And this knowledge will keep you humble when you feel compelled to judge others. Remember where you came from, what you have done, and remember God's mercy." His words reverberated in his mind, echoing an unexpected hope for a soul who had long ago given up on the idea of hope.

"How can you talk of mercy when all of you are facing your death?"

And then Brother Guidrade smiled at him. "Etienne, remember there is no death, just transition. We are all going home."

It was devastating. His experiences, his time among these people, had left him broken apart. All the delusions he'd clung to were ripped away, leaving in their wake a mentality that, in truth, was still evolving. They had ruined him, reformed him, left him raw, but now irrevocably filled with unfathomable possibilities.

Etienne knew that Brother Guidrade believed what he said. But he wasn't at all sure that he could. He had faced so many dangers throughout the years but could say with all honesty that he was completely terrified of this rite. He fully and perhaps rightly expected his sin-ridden life to burn him up into cinders when the ceremony began.

But as it was, it didn't. The details, of course, he would never reveal.

There were vows taken that he would always honor. And there was also the light, a burning white light shining everywhere, illuminating all the shadows around him. Perhaps that is what truth is the burning away of illusion — a painful thing to have all self-deception stripped away. And for a time and in memory, he understood. He was spirit, and this spirit was connected to something greater than himself. And every thought and action of his would cause a ripple in the universe and a connective reaction. This he understood and accepted completely.

And when it was over, and the ceremony was completed, Etienne was weeping. It was a rare and strange thing for him to weep, something he had believed belonged to another lifetime. For so long, he had allowed himself to be cold and removed, insulated from emotion, pain, and connection, perhaps. But then he understood truly in that moment what was truth and what was meaningless, and he wept.

And he asked, some time afterward, about Brother Claude. How could he possibly undergo such a rite, such a profound initiation, and then betray?

Brother Guidrade seemed reflective at the question and did not answer right away. But he could see pain in his eyes. He had instructed Claude in the teachings of the people from a young age.

"Brother Claude has punished himself for his betrayal. It had only been a year since he had taken the initiation, too short a time. Breaking his vows in such a calamitous fashion has unleashed a terrible effect upon him. He will call it a curse, but we understand it is only the effect of his action. The consolamentum is designed to separate the spirit from the flesh to make the transition easier. For Brother Claude, it has become twisted and will wreak a terrible and painful existence for him."

He listened carefully, hearing pain and sympathy in Brother Guidrade's voice that he could not share. He supposed that, in many ways, he was unworthy, for he still harbored the fire of hatred deep within his heart.

03

"What does that mean?" she asked in a panicked tone.

He stood up and walked over to the couch, sitting beside her. Picking up her hand without a word, he put his fingers directly on her racing pulse. "You're much too upset about all of this, Noel."

"What do you mean, he can look like anybody?"

He continued to hold her wrist, trying consciously to send some calming energy to her, another little trick he'd picked up from the Cathars. "What I mean is that Claude and I have crossed paths since Montségur several times, and each time —"

"Each time?" she repeated.

"Each time," he said quietly, "he looks different."

She took a long pause, and he waited, allowing the conversation to unfold at her pace. "You mean he was in disguise?"

He shook his head, fully understanding how implausible his words sounded. But then again, his very existence was implausible. "No, I mean he had a different body."

"You mean possession?"

"Perhaps, I'm not really sure at all how he does it. That was one reason why I needed a seer, someone who can track his essence to wherever it is now. In the past, I was able to use other means."

Her face was pale, and her eyes wide with what he concluded was a measure of horror. "And I still don't understand why it is me."

He nodded slowly, "Yes, I don't either, Noel. But I knew as soon as I met you that, for some reason, it was. And your dream only confirms this. Regardless of how threatening Claude had made himself, contact has been made."

Again, she shook her head, expressing with mounting agitation, "It's too much." Perhaps, it wasn't fair. Perhaps, he was taking advantage, but just now, there was no help for it. There was a thread here, a tenuous thread connecting everything.

"Yes," he coaxed in the most soothing voice he could muster at such a moment, "unfortunately, life doesn't go according to plan. Instead reveals and compels at its own rate. Best, I suppose to see where it leads us."

She focused on him with an expression that told him distinctly she did not share his philosophy. "I've no idea what to do here."

He nodded, squeezing her wrist a bit. "Well, the easiest thing would be to find Claude as quickly as possible so you can get on with your life."

She leaned back against the sofa, closing her eyes and sighing deeply. "Oh yes, I have a wedding to plan."

"So, how about a bit of meditation?"

"What do you have in mind?" she murmured, eyes still closed, but he could feel her relaxing. At the very least, he could feel her pulse rate slowing a bit.

"Let's keep it simple. Now that you've met Claude, simply focus on him, his essence, and see if you can pick up anything."

She nodded, eyes still closed and head resting on the back of the sofa. But he could feel a shift, a shift in energy that was perceptive to his skin. He was a creature greatly tied to the earth, so his awareness was always grounded in very primal sensations. "I'll anchor you," he added, for there wasn't really anything else for him to do. He wasn't a seer, but Noel clearly was. That much he could feel now as she reached outward.

"How old are you?" she whispered as she sunk deeper into her transient state.

"Very old, very, very old," he responded with no elaboration.

9.

Brother Claude

Learning

One would think, having lived on the earth across the span of over five hundred years, that great wisdom would be amassed.

Well, one thing that should be acknowledged is that more time is not necessarily time used wisely. Sometimes it's just more — more to while away. Yes, of course, more to revel in and experience and hopefully learn.

But as in my case, I've come to understand that great learning is not necessarily accomplished over a great stretch of accumulating knowledge.

More often than not, real learning happens in a nuance, in a crystallized moment of clarity of realization, like a tiny treasure — a teardrop of a diamond, so easily missed, so easily unrecognized if you're not paying attention.

And for someone like me who has lived so long and admittedly has become quite adept at wasting time, I've been guilty of not paying *attention and almost allowing those nuances of genuine learning to slip away unnoticed — almost, that is.*

1244 AD

The time after Montségur fell became a strange sort of void for him. In some ways, he was numb, in others hollow, but in the most important ways, he was lost. From the heights of the castle, the remaining garrison and the three other Perfects that were hidden with him watched the smoke rise at a distance.

Brother Guilleme, chosen in final moments that made it impossible for him to protest, moaned and fell to his knees, passing into unconsciousness. In those dark and terrible moments, Etienne couldn't deny that the consolamentum had left him altered but altered in ways he didn't fully understand.

He felt pain and fear rise in him so powerful that it seemed as though it would engulf him completely. And then there was something else on its heels, on the fringes, just beyond understanding. He felt release, pure release, and then finally a whisper in his mind from Brother Guidrade, who he knew definitively as he knew his own skin had already departed from the flesh.

"Stay strong, stay true, Brother Etienne, and you will find what you seek."

The remainder of the dark day fell into a gray haze that had wrapped itself over his mind and body like a protective fog. It was too much to take in, so he simply shut down.

Young Brother Guilleme came to consciousness again and spoke little, simply readying himself for the mission at hand.

And deep in the night, with ropes and tools crafted by the people in secret, they four, the remaining Perfects and another soldier, descended the sheer drop off the Northwest corner of the mountain of Montségur.

CB

It was foolish.

She'd learned of meditation from her mother, practiced it with her sisters, and knew intrinsically that specific preparations had to be made. One endeavoring to travel on an astral plane truly must have a firm hold on their circumstance and achieve a certain stability of mind. All these things she knew, but at the moment, in a decision of panic, had brushed such considerations aside. And that would be her downfall.

She felt herself drawn quickly, quickly, and without her own volition to a place she'd seen in her dreams the day before. And her heart dropped profoundly at the realization. It was the dimly lit interior chamber at the castle of Montségur not so very different from the dream the previous night. Her goal had been thwarted, and again she was sucked into the construction of another's making.

"So soon, my dear, I'm flattered."

A chill passed through her, and she realized that, again, she was only dressed in the thin white shift and that she hurt all over as if she'd only just dragged herself through the crumbling tunnel. It was obvious that she'd completely lost control of this process. "This isn't—"

"What you intended? Clearly not, nor did you or Brother Etienne choose to heed my warning." It was the same as it had been. He dressed in long dark robes, face eerily pale in the flickering torchlight. Only he seemed closer to her now. In fact, he was standing directly in front of her, speaking to her face so that she could feel his cool breath touch her cheek.

57

"Well, that's almost correct."

It was shocking, certainly unexpected — that familiar voice emanating from behind her. But when she slowly turned around, what she saw was impossible, breaking all the rules of meditation. But here he was with her, instead of behind at the house anchoring her in this endeavor. Definitely Ethan Garraint, but dressed differently — in some sort of antiquated tunic and trousers with a huge crossbow strapped to his back. "I thought you were staying behind." She couldn't help but say with evident distress. How had he managed this?

His eyes were not even looking at her, just fixed securely on Claude Barraud. Even from her distance and in the dim flickering torchlight, she could see that they blazed in anger in a way she had never seen before. "Didn't trust Brother Claude here. Although I can't really understand why you continue to gravitate to this place, Brother, the scene of your downfall."

"Some would say it was the scene of my greatest success. Singlehandedly, I brought the holy ones to their knees," the voice was hollow of emotion. She felt keenly and with no reason to support it that he didn't believe what he was saying. Clearly, he was goading Ethan, a game, just a game, she thought. "You should give up this vendetta, Etienne." Again, he spoke with little inflection, but their voices felt distinct, as though they were echoing in the chamber or perhaps in her head.

Ethan moved closer to them — to her and Claude Barraud, who now literally seemed inches from her. "I wonder what all the Perfects that died in flames not so far from this spot would have to say about your great success. Your betrayal of their faith." His voice was cold, but she could feel the nearly uncontrollable anger ready to explode from beneath.

Claude, who stood now before her but also nearly at the center of the gleaming mosaic floor, answered quietly. "Perhaps not at all what you might expect. They would not waste their time indulging in vengeance the way you do. It is a wonder to me, given your disposition, that you could take the consolamentum with no adverse repercussions."

"I did not betray a whole culture — the family that raised you when you had no one."

The sounds, the voices, the emotion were actually in her head, painfully loud as if she was caught, no, trapped in the crossfire. "Do not presume to know my soul Etienne when it is so blatantly clear that you are obtusely disconnected from your own."

The hatred seethed from Ethan. She could see it like a red-hot raging glow that engulfed him. "And what did they offer you, Brother? To betray your own people? You've never told me."

"At the time, freedom," he whispered, "power." But Noel could feel the emptiness of his words, as though he had rattled off something that had no meaning.

"I see," Ethan said, moving closer beside her. She felt sick, physically sick. The rage was simply permeating from him. "No doubt, well worth all the innocent blood you have on your hands. But now you have the choice to make amends."

Finally, Noel felt some genuine emotion stirring in the cold man beside her. "Amends, you say, and how exactly do you propose I accomplish this?"

There was silence, and she wondered for a time if Ethan would answer at all, but then finally, he did. His voice was low, controlled, but precise. "That's simple. Surrender yourself to me, Claude Barraud."

He stirred beside her, the man in the long black robes. "I see. Throw myself on your mercy."

"No, Brother, there is no mercy for you here. Allow me to execute you as you allowed all those innocent souls to be executed so long ago. And finally, end your miserable existence."

There was silence but tension so palpable in the archaic chamber that she felt it was reverberating off the smooth stone walls.

Then finally, Claude responded with little inflection. "Well, that is an interesting offer, but I think, given the circumstances, that I will make one of my own."

There seemed an endless stretch of quiet, and, for a moment, she felt as though nothing would happen. Then out of nowhere, Noel felt a sharp, excruciating pain wrap around her chest, squeezing the breath straight out of her. "I can't afford to have you trailing me through history like some mentally deficient Flying Dutchman. So, I ask you now, Brother, how many innocents are you willing to see destroyed at the feet of your vendetta?"

Again, she felt a powerful squeeze in her chest, so sharp, so acute that she cried out, falling to her knees. She could feel Ethan's hands grasping her shoulders. "Claude, stop this now," he rasped in anger.

"No, Brother," he said calmly. "This is for you to stop. Stop before more, as you call them, innocents fall."

And then she felt the pull, the air shift, and her soul rushing painfully back to her body.

ᚼ

There was a point, an indistinguishable point when Noel slipped from the meditation into the darkness of unconsciousness. It was the moment when the last tatters of her control snapped, but the visions did not — rather, they became more vivid and even less controlled.

The chamber around her had dissipated entirely as she walked through the gleaming halls of somewhere quite unexpected. Of course, it was empty, expansive, cold, and echoing quite exactly what she would expect the New Orleans Museum of Art to feel like if it were completely devoid of occupants, although she had never been inside it when it was in such a state.

She glanced down, still barefoot, dressed in that white shift, as she made her way through the main gallery and began slowly ascending the grand staircase at the back of the main showroom.

She didn't know where she was headed, not really. Her feet simply moved insistently of their own volition. The great white walls around her, usually quite packed with exhibits, were now strangely blank. But her disconnected mind didn't take much time to acknowledge that fact. She simply allowed herself to be drawn onward, more or less powerless to stop it — now on the second floor, walking deliberately towards another staircase. This one not so grand but made largely of glass. She knew it led up to the third floor, and as her feet touched the first step, she was shocked by the nearly icy contact.

൭

Her eyes snapped open abruptly. She drew a deep breath that felt acutely painful within her chest. Ethan sat beside her squeezing her hand. "Are you all right, Noel?" his voice sounded highly agitated, not at all his usual smooth tones.

Vision was still swimming, but she tried hard to focus — again, another breath and a sharp stab within her chest. Then she remembered the chamber at Montségur and the pain she'd felt.

She tried shallow breathing. It was easier. "It hurts," she managed to get out.

He stood up in front of her, still holding her hand. "I'm sorry, Noel. This is my fault."

10.

A Different Footing

1244 AD

"There's the capacity for light and darkness in all of us. You should know that better than anyone Brother Etienne."

There was often a suggestion among the Cathars, particularly the Perfects, that his true lycanthrope nature was known — at times intimated but never explicitly pronounced.

He sat in the courtyard with Brother Guidrade deep in the center of the castle of Montségur. The castle, as it was termed, was more like a fortress with high walls surrounding them that had protected the people quite well until now.

Around them were the inhabitants, once occupants of that lovely village outside the walls, huddled together everywhere — sitting in groups, trying to rally each other's spirits, mostly in clothes tattered and unwashed due to the tight rationing of water. At this point, the cisterns of water had been sabotaged, as well as the eastern barbican of the castle being taken, opening up a pivotal vulnerability. And they knew the Perfecti knew who was responsible for all this with no direct knowledge. For that was the way of the people — the ability to connect to a pool of universal knowledge and energy.

"How can you consider having mercy toward Barraud?" He refused to call him Brother, although most of the Perfecti still did. He couldn't comprehend their tolerance.

"It's not a question of mercy Brother Etienne. You remember the inquisitor who bore your name?"

"Yes, of course." He sighed deeply. Two inquisitors in Avignonet, one to his chagrin bearing the name Etienne, were overtaken by a band of Cather supporters after having killed, tortured, and slaughtered so many of the Credenti.

"Do you believe he was unredeemable?"

"Of course, although I imagine you are going to tell me he was not."

"Every soul Etienne has the capability of being purified and returning to its maker."

"Everyone is redeemable, then you say?"

"As long as the spirit remains, there is hope."

And he looked at the elder Cathar Perfect with a bit of confusion. "What if it doesn't, the spirit, I mean, leaves."

He sighed deeply, "Yes, that is most sad. But it does happen when it senses no purpose in remaining."

※

They didn't speak for some time, although he'd brought her a cup of tea that Noel sipped silently. It wasn't as if she didn't have anything to say. It was literally that she had no energy to speak. The entire episode had sucked everything out of her.

Ethan had been in and out of the room, sometimes staring out the window, sometimes sitting quietly, not really watching, rather seeming lost in his own thoughts — and other times absent altogether.

And then, finally, he settled back into the large rocking chair not far from the sofa. "Are you feeling any better?" he asked.

She breathed in and felt a sharp pain around the area of her ribs. "I'm shaky but better, I think. I'd like to go home."

"You should go home and rest," he said rather firmly.

She nodded, staring at him a bit blankly. "And then?"

His eyes seemed odd to her, very focused and direct — not at all the smooth, charming fellow she'd met on the Lakefront. This was a different side of Ethan Garraint, a more formidable side, she thought. "You should rest. You're out of this now, Noel."

It took a moment for his words to sink in fully. "Out of this? What does that mean?"

"It means it's become too dangerous for you," he stated flatly. "I don't want your help anymore."

Her spine stiffened a bit against the softness of the sofa. It was odd. She felt conflicted. After all, this was what she'd wanted, to be left alone and go back to her life. But at the same time, it was irritating. "So, what are you going to do about Claude Barraud?"

His face remained stern, but she noted the slightest look of surprise cross his features. Evidently, he'd expected her to grab her walking papers and run, which was precisely what she should do. Why she wasn't doing it was a bit confusing even to herself. "I'll just have to find another way to find him."

She shook her head, "And that's it?"

"It's for the best, Noel," he stated quietly but emphatically.

She waited for more, more elaboration, more anything. But there was nothing except the glint of determination in his eyes.

11.

THE EARTH'S LIVING ENERGY

The City

The city smells like living — all manner of living from the lowest, most abhorrent form to the most evolved. Yes, oddly enough, even souls deeply akin to those I encountered in the Pyrenees, those seeking whole-heartedly reconnection to the divine spirit and release from the materialistic earthly plane.

And where do I fit in? The Cathari taught me that every living thing has a purpose. That even my life — as unorthodox as it might be — has a reason for being.

Sometimes I ponder it. Sometimes I ignore it. Maybe I'm a witness to the evolution or de-evolution, if you will, of the planet. At times and in the flicker of a moment, I feel as though I can just grasp it.

And then it eludes me like a wisp of smoke, a phantom, water slipping through my fingers — an illusion.

But enough with the metaphors — the city of New Orleans. I have a yin/yang relationship with it. At times, I've admired its lovely *level of indulgence. And at other moments, it repels me — a problematic relationship, but then again, what relationship had I ever had that was not just so.*

I could understand, however, why Brother Claude had gravitated here. The souls in this city were, at the very least, alive, pulsating with life force — something he desperately needed to exist, to maintain even a facsimile of living.

ଓ

He prowled. That is the only way he could describe it to anyone who has not lived inside his skin. He went deep into the city after night had fallen, into its heart. For every person, every location in the world has an active beating heart. And for New Orleans, this was the French Quarter, not geographically a particularly large area, a graph of streets bordered abruptly on one side by the living, flowing waters of the Mississippi River. It was an acreage of territory marked by generations, literally centuries of living. And it pulsated with it, for good or ill and most times, as had been in his observance, for both.

It was Friday night, around nine in the evening, and the Quarter swarmed with activity — clubs, restaurants, gatherings, all manner of activity. And he silently walked the streets, letting himself drop down into an instinctual realm. He had no way of knowing where Claude Barraud would be, but his skin, his senses, told him one simple fact that he craved.

What exactly Barraud craved still eluded him. But one could not live off the earth as an immortal without feeding on something. For him, it was the very earth itself, strong points of energy emanating from its very core, which strangely enough powered this area.

He continued to walk, the boots that he'd tripped about in not so many months before, through the mountains of the Appalachians, hitting the often cracked and uneven pavement. He allowed himself to feel the pull and set the wolf free. If he had been elsewhere, he would have transformed. There was no help for it. The urge was so strong, but in the midst of the well-populated streets, it was impossible. But he did so within his soul. Thought became animalistic, and he moved as the hunter through the concrete terrain.

ལ

"Noel."

She sat up and looked across the darkened bedroom.

A chill traveled across her bare skin as her eyes focused on the empty place on the bed beside her. She had expected, and then she stopped. Patrick, she remembered. He'd come over tonight, but oddly now, her mind was blurred, confused. Had he? Hadn't he been with her here tonight?

She stood up in the darkness and pulled on a silky white robe to cover her, yes, her nakedness. Of course, he'd been here. It was not her custom to sleep in the nude. She remembered now, although it was broken. He'd held her in his arms so close.

He'd shown up late tonight, very late. And she'd been surprised because he'd told her quite explicitly earlier that he had a late dinner meeting. It had bothered her, the meeting. It hadn't been the first, and she was ashamed to say her suspicious nature thought perhaps it wasn't a meeting at all. But that was the way of their relationship. She was always a bit off balance, always a bit unsettled.

But then she'd done again what she'd become quite accomplished at. She swept the doubts aside, swept the uneasi-

69

ness away. In only six months, they would be married, and all those nagging questions would seem ridiculous. Clearly, it was just a product of an unsettled mind. After all, she'd been through hell today.

Then later, quite late after she'd gone to bed, there was a knock at her door. It was odd. Patrick usually called. But there he was at her door, silently watching her. He was dressed in a dark suit — one she didn't recall and then dramatically and rather romantically, he'd pulled her into his arms.

"Remember we said we'd wait," agreed upon abstinence, at least for a bit, until the wedding. But he didn't acknowledge that. Literally, he'd scooped her quite off her feet and taken her into the bedroom, where they'd made love passionately.

Her heart slammed at the memory. It was intense and strangely different from the times before. Almost as if he was starved for her. Not like the Patrick she remembered, although granted, it had been several months. Maybe the waiting had gotten to be too much for him. But he had always been calmer, not so intense, not so, dare she say, determined — not like this time. This time her mind and body swirled in pleasure as though something had been released, tapped into. It had brought her hope in a curious way. Perhaps this marriage would be less predictable than she'd thought.

She felt another chill sweep over her as she entered the apartment's den. It was a warm night, but of course, she wasn't wearing anything beneath the light robe.

There he stood. He hadn't left as she, for a fleeting moment, had thought. He stood, his back to her, staring out the sliding glass doors onto the back patio. She began to walk toward him and then stopped.

Her heart clutched in confusion. It was the same dark suit, and he was the right height, with dark hair. But a realization, a cold, austere realization, crept into her. And he turned around slowly. Her breath had fled. The face was cold but the same as in the dream, in the chamber at Montségur with Ethan Garraint. He smiled, and dread filled her. How could it be? How could she have?

"Noel," he whispered in her mind. "Now you belong to me."

She sat up in the bed, out of breath. She glanced around frantically. She was alone, and it had been a dream. But as she stretched her hand out next to her, she could feel the empty place in the bed was still warm.

☙

It was an old building, a hotel, that he walked into. But he felt the pull like a rope around him.

"Let yourself feel Etienne, the pull of the earth's living energy. It will power you and allow you to gain mastery over your nature."

The lobby was milling with people, some good, most in between. It was easiest when he was in this mode to feel the makeup of souls— the energy they emit.

It wasn't at all preordained. The soul was part of one's being that is new, blank. It is dyed any color by one's actions in their lifetime.

And he could feel the bands, the auras colliding from all the people around him. But he pushed on, walking across the long stretch of polished floor, right to the end of the impossibly long room near the elevators. There was a curving staircase where without missing a beat, he began to descend rapidly.

☙

"Close your eyes."

"No," she rasped. Her heart was beating wildly. She didn't know what was happening. What was real and what could not be.

"Noel," a soft, compelling voice just in her mind. "It's all right." It strove to comfort, but she could not allow it.

"What are you doing? What are you doing to me?"

"Relax, Noel. There is no reason to fear me. Now we are bonded."

"No," she whispered, trying to fight but feeling a sleepiness flood over her.

"There is no reason to resist me. I need your help now."

And she began to dream.

ଓ

It was here long before anyone thought to build a city, long before man put his imprint on the earth. He descended the stairs, his feet almost rebounding in excitement.

But here below was quiet, nearly deathly quiet in stark contrast to the raucous atmosphere up above. There was a long narrow hall and closed-off rooms, offices, he supposed. But he didn't see this, not at all. He walked onward, feeling the energy, strong old energy bouncing off everywhere.

If he'd truly been alone, Ethan Garraint would have been more than comfortable pulling off all his clothes and allowing his bones to meld shape, his body to mutate freely into the animal. He craved it. In that state, he would feel the full effects of all the powerful energy bands. But instead, he dropped to the ground and crossed his legs, pulling open his shirt and exposing his heart, as he had done in meditation so long ago in the home of the Cathari. He breathed deeply and felt renewal, the powerful energy pouring upward through the earth and nearly tearing at him until it reached his very core.

12.

THE THIRD FLOOR

1244 AD

"How do you know that all of this was not meant to be?"

He'd returned. He shouldn't have. He had been warned against it by Brother Guilleme and Brother Arnaud, the two other surviving Perfects who had aided him in their last mission for the Cathari. They had warned him not to return, but he did — only a month after the siege had ended. It was still occupied, the castle fortress but by a skeletal garrison. So, in the night, he had ascended the South side of the plateau with its treacherous rocky path and hairpin turns that his feet knew so well, recognizing them intimately even in the darkness. He had no idea what he hoped to gain but instead followed the wild drive within him.

Most was in shadow. It was clear that the few remaining soldiers hired by the papacy were not housed within the castle as he and his comrades had been. Instead, no doubt, they had commandeered the houses that the Credenti once occupied. It angered him thinking of those dwellings now spoiled and desecrated by the very people responsible for the Cathar's destruction. But he continued, taking the secret pathway that cut beneath the fortress walls into their sacred chamber — the chamber where he'd taken the vows of the consolamentum.

Even before Etienne crossed the threshold, he saw the light emanating from within. Even before he went inside, he smelled Barraud, his stench. He would no doubt be outnumbered if he pursued this. Barraud wouldn't be so foolish as to be alone. He should wait and turn back, but then again, he didn't know when he would have another opportunity like this to dispatch the traitor.

As he crept into the chamber, he recognized rather quickly that he was wrong. Barraud, indeed was there, standing at the center of the room but completely alone.

He seemed lost in his thoughts, but after a moment, he raised his head and focused his gaze on a man he once called Brother. He spoke slowly, "You're foolish, Etienne to return here."

His hand fell on the knife he had strapped to his side. "Perhaps," he said, moving deliberately closer.

His intent, his whole intent, was to lunge the dagger deep into Claude's heart. But then, as he began to approach, Barraud quickly reached down, picking up a sword that evidently had been lying at his feet. "You see, I knew you were coming. My time with the Cathari was not wasted." He pointed the sword at him, but Etienne was still just yards away, close enough to get in some sort of strike. "Don't you want to ask me why?" Barraud said with a confidence that only fueled Etienne's anger.

"No, I am not here for your words."

"Then I ask you Brother, Brother Etienne, who has appointed himself my executioner. I ask you, Brother, how do you know? How do you know that this was not God's plan all along to have me play the fallen angel, to play Lucifer the great betrayer? That I am not only a pawn."

The words all bounced off of him, unabsorbed. There was no explanation for what Barraud had done, no possible excuse worth entertaining even for a moment. "If that is so, then it is my role to dispatch you, to avenge all those innocent souls." He said this quietly, for he believed it purely.

"Innocent?" he answered, waving the sword about dramatically in exaggeration. And he'd felt it at that moment, felt acutely his nemesis' desperation. In his bones, he felt there was something already pressing in on Claude, exacting its toll. "They've gone home to their God."

"And you sent them there, just as if you'd pushed them into the fire."

"Are you sure, Etienne? You don't know me."

"And I will not. I only live now to see your blood spilled."

With his sword still pointing at Etienne's heart, Barraud stepped back and yelled, not unexpectedly. "Guards, now."

Of course, there was no surprise here. Barraud was a coward. Three well-armed men with swords and spears entered through the northern entrance. Etienne jumped back, allowing his rage to consume him as he willed the transformation. There was no need for the power of the full moon. For some time, he had mastered the process, using it at will. His very skin began tearing off his bones as his structure shifted. The searing pain mutated into wild exhilaration as his mind sunk into the animal. The animal literally began to tear, ripping the flesh of the soldiers. Of course, Barraud had already escaped, leaving behind others to bear the consequences of his heinous acts.

∞

After a time, he stirred, slowly opening his eyes. The memory had come to him so clearly, so tangible. It was almost as though he were there again. And it had come for a reason, coupled with understanding — one more piece of what he needed to know. Claude Barraud as well sought the renewal of energy. That was why he had returned to Montségur. Already, he was feeling the burden of his actions.

❧

She breathed in deeply, the cool air of the museum. It seemed late, probably near closing. She did work late from time to time at the museum, but usually, it was for an event, a fund-raising party, or perhaps the private debut of an exhibit for museum members. But if this were the case, there would be people, not as it was now, not deserted.

Her eyes slowly scanned the second floor. All she felt was dizziness and disorientation. Noel glanced down. She wore her work clothes — dress pants, white blouse, and dark blue blazer. But her mind was clouded. She couldn't remember coming to work this morning.

She reached the glass staircase on the second floor leading up to the third, again a profound sweep of dizziness and disorientation. The exhibits up there were fixed, so she had little need to venture there. And as it was, it always affected her. The third floor was almost an Anthropology Museum with Ancient and Primitive Art — strange artifacts from South America and Africa: masks, totems, sculptures, and other ornamental items. But for her and evidently her family, it was problematic. Her mother told her it was the energies. Josephine had experienced the very same reaction whenever she'd come to the museum. Noel had been taught long ago that objects often absorbed and held the powerful energies created around them.

So, she rested her hand on the cool metal banister digging in with determination to resist where she was being prodded to go. She felt confused, and the outside pressure to continue was enormous. Distantly, she could hear the footsteps behind her, but her concentration remained within. And then she felt a cool hand cover hers. She looked up into the eerily pale green eyes, and her heart sunk. Of course, this wasn't real. It was some sort of dream.

"Who is to say what is real, Noel, and what is not? But however you choose to look at it, this will not do."

"What do you mean?" she whispered, understanding now that the pressure she felt to go to the third floor came solely from him.

Claude smiled, and oddly she found it compelling. How could she be drawn to him, all that he was? "I need your help, Noel. I need you to help me find what I seek. Up there." And he motioned with his hand pointing upward. Some passersby might think perhaps that he was referring to the heavenly realm. But she knew quite succinctly that he was only indicating the third floor.

1242 AD

"I'm not sure that I understand completely this concept of the spirit and the soul."

There were a handful of conversations that he could remember having with Brother Claude long before his betrayal, before his infamy. On this particular day, they were sitting outside of the castle, which was firmly on a rocky spur within the heart of the Pyrenees surrounded by sheer cliffs. They had settled out a bit, perched on a precipice overlooking the deep expanse of the surrounding valley below. It might have seemed precarious to some, but he'd noted Brother Claude had a side to him, an edge, if you will, that flirted with danger regardless of how pious he might seem at times.

He sighed deeply, "Well, Brother, as I was taught, the spirit is old, created in heaven. It reincarnates many times and lives through many souls. In contrast, the soul is fresh, young, and unique to each lifetime. It connects the spirit to the body, and the spirit connects both to the eternal."

"Is it possible to possess a soul and no spirit?" He wasn't sure what prompted him to ask such a thing, just a question that presented itself spontaneously in his mind. Of course, the people had taught him there were no accidents. If the question occurred, it was sent for a reason, with a relevance that would be revealed in its proper time.

And at that, Brother Claude had laughed shortly, which at the moment had seemed somewhat inappropriate and surprised him. "Let's see, a soul with no connection to the divine. Yes, Brother, there have been cases when the spirit abandons the soul prematurely."

"Abandons?"

"Indeed, we are given only a certain amount of time on this earth, our physical bodies. Of course, that time varies. But the spirit has a blueprint of learning, learning that can be derailed by individual choice, free will if you like. So, when a person falls too far off course, the spirit can give up and return to its home."

"And what happens to the soul?"

"It lives aimlessly and without purpose, no longer guided until its time for death — sad, empty, hollow sort of life."

"And that's all?"

"Yes, I suppose, unless, of course, some other spirit has a use for the shell."

13.

POSSESSION

"What is it, Noel?"

Her mother had arrived at her apartment early in the morning, just as she was getting ready for work. The night before was somewhat chaotic in her mind, a mix of dreams and something else — something else that she couldn't quite solidify into concreteness. She smiled and shook her head. It was all about focusing, focusing on the present, on her plans, on her life. "Nothing, I'm just tired. I've stopped helping Mr. Garraint."

Josephine Duverje was looking at her oddly, an expression Noel was intimately familiar with from childhood. She stood in the middle of her kitchen watching her as though she was some sort of detective sizing up a potential suspect. "I don't understand," she said slowly. "He seemed so emphatic."

She sat down at her small espresso-colored kitchenette table, sipping a cup of hot tea she'd prepared only moments before. "He changed his mind. That's all."

Her mother's dark eyes widened. She was so perceptive. It was a skill that she possessed that her daughter found at times intensely unnerving. "Something's not right here, Noel."

"No, Mom, everything's fine," she explained rather calmly, somewhat surprising herself. "I've just spent some time sorting out my priorities. It's time to get on with life."

Again, her mother stared at her with wide brown eyes that seemed determined to ferret out some truth that she didn't have the energy to provide. "How's Patrick?" she asked carefully.

Noel looked at her a bit blankly. "I'm meeting him for lunch."

ભ

Her office was down a long echoing hallway at the very back of the first floor of the museum. She struggled through a pile of paperwork that had evidently built up over the last few days. Time clearly had not stopped on the outside. Although in the strange world, she'd been moving in, she'd felt quite detached.

But once her mother had left that morning, Noel had decided quite firmly that it was time to get back to the real world — the world where paychecks mattered, where weddings needed to be arranged, where werewolves and vendettas against supernatural villains were only stuff of the imagination.

A perceptible chill swept around her, which wasn't unusual for this area of the museum. It was a tremendous and often drafty building with impossibly high ceilings and persistent whispers from works of art that had been on the earth for many centuries before she had. But these kinds of thoughts she must sweep away. She was determined now to be free, to block out those parts of her life that made her feel weak and out of control.

Concentrating fully, she slowly began to fill out a form on her desk concerning the transfer of an upcoming collection from North Carolina. She breathed in deeply, forcing focus. After all, she'd decided it had been a dream — that unprecedented, nocturnal encounter with the man she'd thought was Patrick. All of it, undeniably, had been a dream. Although when she'd arisen the following day, her body felt distinctly as though she'd made love. But it wasn't possible, and even in speaking to Patrick that morning, he'd related how he'd had a late meeting and then gone to bed just after midnight. There had been no visits from him in the night, not from him. She forcibly pushed it out of her mind. It wasn't something she could consider.

Again, Noel drew a deep breath and felt the coolness of the air around her enter her lungs. She thought they must have the air conditioner higher than usual today. Then another consideration filtered in — perhaps a quick stroll through the museum might help clear away the cobwebs.

She left her office, walking slowly down the long hallway leading to the museum's main showroom. It was a palatial construction with a ceiling that arched up over two stories and great white columns designed, she supposed, to look a bit like the Parthenon supporting the gallery surrounding the second floor. Without any thought, she began to ascend the stairs, and it suddenly felt hauntingly familiar. Of course, she'd done this a thousand times, working here for the past two years, but that wasn't it. It went deeper.

The dream returned, the dream where she'd climbed the stairs, just as she was doing now. Reaching the landing, she turned the corner and saw the other staircase, just a few yards down a long-extended hall. She hesitated. Here, it felt even much cooler than in the rest of the museum, nearly chilled, she thought, as the air brushed the exposed skin on her arms. She'd worn a short-sleeve silky black blouse with a white skirt today. One of the ladies at the front desk, Madeline Lecour, had laughed calling her domino. But now she was cold. There was a light sweater back at her desk that she should retrieve. Her mind counseled this, but she continued to walk, walk until she reached the glass staircase.

It came back to her strongly, profoundly now. She remembered him standing there, from the dream, of course. What had Ethan called him? Claude Barraud had stood there by the staircase in front of her, smiling and then pointing upward to the third floor.

"It makes me dizzy."

"Yes, I know, that's a psychic reaction. I feel it as well."

"Why? What is it?"

"Something up there, something very powerful and very old." Her mother had told her.

Her eyes followed the staircase up to the landing on the floor above. There were things she needed to do. To catch up on important work, a desk full of papers she remembered. She really didn't want to go up there at all, not to the third floor. It wasn't what she wanted at all. These were the thoughts she entertained as she began the ascent.

⋈

"Something is terribly wrong with her."

Ethan sipped a cup of hot coffee as he noted Josephine's cup lay untouched on his table. She'd arrived this morning unannounced, which he thought with some amusement quite echoed her daughter's behavior just the morning before.

"I'm sure Noel told you I no longer require her assistance."

She paced the floor of his den with expanding agitation. It was unusual for her. All his exposure to Noel's mother had demonstrated that she was quite a controlled woman who held her emotions firmly in check. But now, now he was sensing panic.

"You must try to calm yourself, Josephine, and tell me exactly what has led you to this conclusion."

"This morning, I just felt as though it was important to see her, a feeling," then she stopped pacing in front of the stone fireplace and turned to look at him directly. "Or rather a premonition of something. I dropped by her apartment, and I knew immediately that something was off."

"Off?" he repeated.

"Yes, you must understand that I can feel my children, their energy, their aura, their frequency if you like."

He nodded, "I see."

"And almost at once, I could feel the difference. The balance was gone." She rubbed her hands together as though she was agitated and desperately trying to find the words. "Her energy was different."

He understood the gravity of her concern now. "Was there anything specific that was said, Josephine?"

"No, not specific, but, well, I allowed myself to see with the vision. I wanted to see if there had been a change in her aura."

"And had there been?" he asked with mounting interest.

Her eyes widened with a fear that Ethan could feel tangibly. "Yes, it had changed. It was as though it was being enveloped by a darkness, a dark color surrounding her, seeping into her soul."

It hit him succinctly. How stupid of him. Claude Barraud hadn't given up on Noel at all. In fact, he was moving to possess her.

14.

THE ARTIFACT

There were a few people on the third floor, but to her mind, it was largely deserted. Quiet and deserted like the dream, but then she pushed that aside. In the dream, she hadn't come up here. He, Claude, had wanted her to — had pushed her to, but she hadn't. She'd woken up. Again, the dizziness hit her. She remembered the same feeling every time she came to the third floor, which, granted, was rare. These were permanent exhibits from archaic cultures in India, South America, Asia — very old pottery, sculptures, masks, statues, but all things that didn't concern her.

She wandered slowly from room to room, feeling a growing disorientation — feeling rather than seeing what was before her in those glass cases. And then she stopped. Slowly, she spun around the empty room, the empty, cold, drafty room. She was in the midst of the Central American exhibit, Mayan artifacts. But it was strong, the pull and the repulsion simultaneously. She allowed herself to feel, although she knew she shouldn't. It was unwarranted to open herself, to be vulnerable. Her mind expanded, and she felt the powerful pull, almost like hands reaching out to yank her toward one of the glass cases — stone, ancient stone, and blood flowing from it.

Then she stopped. She shut herself down and closed those doors again that she had moments ago opened. She wouldn't do this.

She breathed in deeply, the cool air struggling to regain control when she saw it from the corner of her eye — a movement behind one of the glass cases. It startled her. She had been quite sure that she was alone. And then again, it moved, a figure in a dark suit moving directly into her line of vision. She blinked her eyes. It couldn't be.

"This is disappointing, Noel," he spoke in that voice, that cold voice from her dreams. And then she remembered his hands on her in the night.

"This isn't possible."

He smiled, and she thought him handsome. What was wrong with her? "What you must come to understand is that anything is possible, my dear." Then he was closer to her, closer, although he hadn't moved at all. "Now, let's try again, Noel. There is something here I need. And you are going to help me find it."

ଔ

"You think this man is after Noel?"

He shook his head. "I don't think I would actually call him a man anymore, Josephine. He and I have gone well beyond that particular designation. But yes, now it seems that he wants something from her."

"I don't understand. Noel was simply to help you find him. Why, now, when she isn't helping you anymore, would he pursue her? To hurt you?"

Now he was the one pacing trying to piece together what was happening. "Yes, that would be one explanation, but it's too easy. Claude Barraud is a complicated creature. From what I can gather, his soul became damaged after his betrayal of the Cathari."

"What do you mean damaged?"

Slowly, he sank down into his rocking chair. The rocking chair he had built with his own hands, imbued with his own energy. "It's complicated. I don't know if I even completely understand what has occurred. From what I can gather, it has something to do with the consolamentum. The rites that the Cathars take."

"Yes, I know to become a Perfect, the priests or priestesses of the order."

"Before that dark day, Josephine, the Brothers, the sisters that would refuse to renounce their faith and thus condemned themselves to death convinced me to take the rites; so that I could help them protect what they most treasured. What they treasured more than their own lives."

Her dark eyes were fixed on him, but he could see them expand in astonishment and then understanding."

"But what can this have to do with Noel, with this Claude Barraud?"

"Claude had also become a priest of the Cathars, taken the most sacred rites reserved for their highest priesthood or those preparing to leave this earth."

"Like the last rites?"

He nodded, "Yes and more. In those cases, it unleashes the spirit and the soul from the earthly flesh. But then Barraud betrayed his vows in the most horrific manner. He betrayed his people, and his soul became corrupted and twisted in form and substance."

"I don't understand, Ethan." Her voice sounded panicked, but it was coming together in his mind.

"He is an immortal, never finding rest but often finding the abandoned flesh of others to inhabit. Bodies whose spirit has left them before their time on this earth is finished."

"I do understand that. There are many on this earth that have been abandoned by their celestial spirit."

"Yes, when the soul diverts too much from the spiritual path, the spirit leaves."

"Yes, rather than suffer its own destruction. But Ethan, Noel has not lost her spirit."

"I know," he said slowly, trying to focus on the strange distorted images that were filtering into his consciousness. "But there is something he needs from her. The first time I met her, I felt a distinct connection to Barraud. But I didn't understand it. I—" Then he stopped and walked over to the fireplace, becoming painfully aware of his culpability in this matter. "I was too focused on my own need, my need for vengeance."

"Vengeance," she murmured. "That does not sound like the path of the Cathari."

"No, no, it isn't. But it seems it is mine."

CS

The breath expelled out of her in a panic. "I can't help you."

He looked at her rather stoically but as though he was not acknowledging what she'd said. "There is much power here, Noel. The Mayans were a mystical people, although from time to time, they did pursue their goals in rather grisly ways. Life, blood, sacrifice, not always successful but useful for my needs."

"Your needs?" she repeated. This was painful to her. The dizziness was growing stronger, and her stomach was painfully nauseated.

"I'm sorry. I know this must be very draining to you. Yes, my needs, there is something here, an artifact, powerful, drenched in the spirit of that people. I need it."

"For what?" she questioned.

He sighed heavily. "So, I can live, truly live again."

෫

"I don't understand what use he has for Noel." The mother was frantic. That much he could feel. But he must focus. He must understand what he'd missed.

"She must have something he wants."

Her eyes widened. "What does that mean? My daughter is young. Yes, somewhat confused about a great many things."

He heard her voice, but he was looking outside of the both of them — focusing on the first time he saw Noel at the Lakefront. "Ethan, are you—"

"Please, one moment Josephine." He said a bit sternly.

He stood at the picture window facing out to the side yard. But he didn't see what was before him. His mind continued to focus completely on their first meeting.

91

He was there again, now, in his mind. Even as he approached her, he could feel her distraction. Power and distraction, so dangerous, so tumultuous. He stopped for a moment, completely absorbing himself in the memory. The room disappeared around him, and again, he was near the water, but this time he hesitated.

Noel was looking forward, not at all aware of his impending approach. He could feel the warmth of the sun overhead, although it was a cloudy day, a stormy day. The sun would appear momentarily and then disappear. He paused deliberately and protracted the time he'd spent before approaching her. Just as he'd studied with the Cathari, he focused forward, absorbing every nuance of vibration. He felt her aura, strong but shrouded, confused as if something was already surrounding it. Then he stopped. It was true that he'd initially felt that she could lead him to Claude Barraud. But even then, he hadn't understood why. He'd assumed, then he stopped. Again, he allowed himself to feel. So subtle, so disguised that no one would see it unless they were looking intently. But he felt his energies already close to her, already having made contact even then, even before then.

He violently yanked himself back to his present circumstance. "Josephine, Noel, is it possible she had contact with Barraud before I even came into the picture?"

She'd been sitting quietly on the couch, evidently well aware that he'd been embarking on a psychic journey of sorts. "Contact? I'm not sure what you mean. In dreams?"

He shook his head slowly. No, that didn't feel quite right. It had to be more tangible. "No, I don't know a new acquaintance six months to a year ago, it seems."

Her eyes widened with concern. "No, I mean, the only one has been Patrick."

15.

BROTHER GUILLEME

Noel had returned to her office and waited quietly, calmly, her limbs feeling as though they were trembling. It was impossible. She was seeing him now in waking hours. She hadn't returned to the third floor, although it had taken her every ounce of fortitude to resist the compulsion. She'd walked away from him feeling drained, weak, desiring nothing more than to do as he wanted — to give him whatever he wanted, no matter the cost.

So, now she sat at her desk motionless when people passed by pretending to work, although her eyes were blurry and her nerves screaming. She simply sat there waiting, waiting for her *fiancé* to arrive to take her to lunch. She would lean on him, although she couldn't possibly tell him what was wrong. But he was strong and solid and would help her combat — nervously, she clasped her hands in front of her — whatever this was.

She didn't hear his approach. She was all too caught up in her own thoughts. But she did feel a warm hand on her shoulder. She glanced up into Patrick's eyes, dark brown eyes, and she smiled with familiarity. "You seem pale," he murmured. "Feeling all right?"

"I don't know," she whispered. "A little under the weather."

He smiled. It was a distant smile. Patrick had an extremely angular face. Some would call it unfinished, not particularly refined, but definitely striking. Memorable, she'd always thought. He was just thirty, and their lives together stretched before her like a golden mirage. "Let's take a walk," he said.

She stood up feeling a bit dizzy, but he supported her with his arm. Something slipped into her. It wasn't exactly energy, not the kind of healing energy she was used to from her mother and sisters. It was something else. Something that made her thinking even cloudier. "I think I'd like to leave."

"In a bit," he whispered, leading her out of the room.

1246 AD Toulouse, France

"What's happening to me?" He reached out, but his fingers felt numb, disconnected. The sense of touch was dissipating.

It had been nearly two years since the fall of Montségur, and Claude Barraud had changed his name to Baron Sournois, living in a comfortable and prosperous estate on the outskirts of the city of Toulouse. It was there, within the city walls, that one day he had spied a familiar face from his past — young Brother Guilleme, who, upon seeing him just froze in his spot upon the cobbled street, staring at Claude. "Brother Claude," he whispered quite in astonishment, it seemed as he was approached.

And it was within this very moment that everything shifted. Claude began to feel the change, the tremors in his body, the lack of sensation in his limbs, and most of all, the pain, pain like fire along his skin.

It was an odd, unfathomable instance not unlike being struck like lightning, but his mind, as it had always been, worked quickly, even under great duress. "Thief, thief!" he yelled, grabbing hold of young Guilleme's shoulders. After all, he was a Baron now, not a man without influence, and so, he had the man that he once called Brother arrested and thrown into the local gaol. It was a place he could be sure to find him, and as it was, he visited him two days later.

The symptoms accelerated rapidly. The pain and the numbness became unbearable, and then there were dreams — dreams of fire where his skin was separating from his soul, and he traveled about lost and disembodied. It was unconscionable that now after he'd made his escape, had prepared his way for a new life of privilege that now he would be struck down in this way. In arrogance and terror, he refused to accept it.

Within the cold quiet of Guilleme's cell, he exploded with rage at the placid young man who seemed more aged than his years accounted for and yet seemingly untouched by his surroundings. Again, he reiterated, "I told you to tell me what is happening, or so help me, I will see you hanged."

Guilleme looked at him with little expression and sat serenely on the one decrepit wooden chair that sat in the corner of the dank, musty cell. "You have killed my people Brother Claude. Do you really believe you can threaten me with anything?"

He breathed deeply. Coherent thoughts were difficult to grasp. It felt like madness. How dare he! How dare he! Didn't he know what he had become, what power he now possessed? But he was like all of them, devoid of respect for anything but their own beliefs. "This did not begin to happen until I laid eyes upon you, Guilleme. Why are you here at all?"

95

"I was sent here, Brother. I was sent here to see you, to bear witness to what you had done."

And then it hit him powerfully, and he felt the air leave his lungs. "This is a curse. You were sent to put a curse on me."

The young man dressed in his shabby, tattered clothes looked at him oddly with a measure of sympathy that only served to enrage him. "No, my Brother, this is no curse. This is simply the consequence of what you have done. You took the rites, the sacred vows of the consolamentum, to purify the soul, to prepare it for the return to the divine. But in breaking those vows, you have twisted its intent. Your soul rejects the material but is unworthy to return to the divine. It is eternal but trapped in this materialistic realm where it will suffer until it can be purified."

The words, the words tore through him. Immortality, cursed, painful immortality, not human, not spirit. "That is barbaric Guilleme, to condemn me."

"No one has condemned you, Brother but yourself. Even now, your soul is tearing away from your body. It will be a struggle to make it stay. You will be a phantom in this world, not really living, unable to die. I would not wish your fate on anyone Brother Claude. May our Creator have mercy on you."

He was horrified, wrapped in his own terror but enraged so much that he nearly leaped across the darkened room to savagely strike Guilleme across the face. But the young man made no sound, just slowly turned back to Claude. "We must all bear the consequences of our choices, Brother."

His hand tingled a bit from the contact, but he could barely feel the sensation within it. The numbness had so set in. "You made a mistake coming here, Guilleme. I will see to it that you die for that mistake." He left, not looking back, but two days later, word came to him that Guilleme had simply vanished from his cell. No one had an explanation, although he did suspect that there were still strong Cathar sympathies beneath the city's surface.

He fought the deterioration for two more years and then found one night that he had abandoned his body while he was unaware. It was then he began to explore the parameters of his cursed existence, dreams, a ghost-like form on the earthly plane, and the power to drain energy from living souls, souls who were unaware. He became a sort of parasite until he discovered the lost ones — the empty bodies walking the earth whose spirits had fled, walking the earth until their allotted time had ended.

Ethan stared at her a bit blankly. "What did you say?" he asked

"I said the only new acquaintance was Patrick, her fiancé."

A slow throb began to beat in his head. Bodies, bodies whose spirits had fled — he'd learned of this long ago.

"Why do they continue?" he'd asked. Then a profound chill ran down his spine, of course, his conversation long ago with Claude himself.

"I don't know. I expect it as a cautionary tale. To remind other souls what happens when they don't pay attention to their spiritual selves. "

"But the souls?"

"No, they don't return to the divine. They sort of deteriorate. We are made of many things, Etienne — spirit, soul, body. None can be ignored."

"The lost ones," he repeated aloud in the present.

"What, what do you mean?" Josephine's voice had reached a bit of a high pitch. It was clear she didn't understand, but she feared.

"That's how Claude continues to survive, inhabits these bodies that have been abandoned by their spirit."

She was standing now just in front of him, breathing deeply. "You think he's made contact with Noel this way? Oh no, you can't think."

"You felt something odd about him, off."

"I felt he wasn't right for her. But she wanted him. Something about him made her feel safe, so I didn't stand — oh my God, you think he's taking over Patrick's body?"

He stared at her, unable to do anything about the horror now reaching her eyes. "No, Josephine, I believe Patrick has been gone for some time now."

16.

PATRICK

"Do you want to walk outside? It might help clear my head."

"No, no, there's something I want to see."

She felt dizzy, oddly as though she were walking in a fog. He had his arm around her and continued to prod her toward the elevator. "What did you want to see?" she asked with confusion.

"Patience," he whispered, then kissed the top of her head. They walked into the elevator, and she nearly felt her knees give way. But he was there again, with his arms around her, sending her energy to calm or make her complacent, she thought disconnectedly. But it was all right because, after all, she didn't want to think. She wanted to lean on him so she didn't have to worry about what was coming, the dread in the back of her mind. It registered when he hit the button to the third floor. "Why do you want to go there?" she asked.

"Don't worry. It's important," was his response. Beneath his words, he said *Trust Me. Trust Me, Noel.* And against those feelings just beyond her hazy grasp, she did.

Cℋℬ

What exactly happened to the soul of Patrick McClure?

Excellent question, but if he could answer that, he could answer what exactly became of the soul of Leon Antoine, Louisa Gans, Andre Francois, Thomas Nolan, Benjamin Scott, and an array of others over the centuries of his peculiar habitation on the earth.

Claude Barraud, although admittedly at times arrogant, did not claim to be privy to the secret machinations of the universe, nor did he consider himself a good soul. He wondered at times why he was not simply condemned to hell for his crimes against an admittedly holy people. But over time, what became clear to him was that hell was different things to different people, not simply a fiery pit of torture but a torture of the psyche often personally tailored to one's individual needs. So, he did all he could. He made the best of his hell, always seeking to escape it or at the least, upgrade it a bit.

What became clear to him as he learned to take up the carcasses of abandoned bodies was that something did remain of the soul. Something departed with the fleeing spirit, but some echo was also left behind. When he first came into contact with Patrick McClure, it was at a somewhat upscale nursing home at the end of Magazine Street. Business had brought him to the city but finding a vehicle, a body, if you will, to inhabit had been more difficult than he had anticipated.

The city itself was deceptive. With the indulgent lifestyles one perceived, the assumption would be that it would be a breeding ground for abandoned bodies. But it was not the case. From what Claude could gather, many spirits settled in the area for great learning, some lessons impossibly destructive but also enlightening. After all, what had the Cathari taught — the more difficult the life, the more purified the soul?

So, for a period of just months, he had taken up an old man's body, his spirit long departed after a lifetime of reckless disregard for the well-being of his fellowman. It was not an easy occupation. The body was riddled with infirmity from years of excess. But for a time, he had no choice. What was left of the old man's soul was already remarkably suppressed, so he easily absorbed it for energy.

And in only two months, during which more than once he'd considered moving on and continuing his search for a more viable vehicle, he had a visitor. It was a young lawyer who, from what fragmented memories he could gather from the old man, managed aspects of his business, a construction company that was now largely run by his sons.

He could smell it immediately. Already the lawyer was a shell, his spirit having fled the year before. But the soul was something else. What remained was clearly the product of quite an ego and an arrogant disposition. The two spoke little at the visit. The lawyer was palpably nervous, bringing papers to sign. But he could see clearly the remnants of his misdeeds in the old man's mind. The young pup had actually arranged a hit for a former employee, threatening to reveal corruption and short-cuts breaking building standards. So, the solution had been simply to make him disappear — a choice no doubt contributing to his present condition.

Sensing the opportunity, he abandoned the old man and followed the lawyer home. The possession took time. As he'd initially detected, the ego was strong and took wearing down. Ambition was the core here. The boy had started as a defender of drunk drivers, a rather unsavory end of the legal profession, and through accommodating ruthless employers, not unlike his last host, ascended to his present position while simultaneously driving his eternal spirit from his body. Within a month, he'd inhabited the shell of Patrick McClure and, for lack of a better word, devoured the shadow that remained of his soul. The body was young, viable, and, unless some catastrophic event ended its existence, would last him a good number of years.

Occupation, of course, wasn't as one would think. He did not live in the body as a human born to the earth. It was more that he rested there and controlled it, oftentimes traveling without. The natural cosmic glue that forged the soul within the body was absent. It was always a temporary fix, one that his goal was to rectify. He narrowed down his target area in a reasonably short time, a very old artifact of great power and energy that he was blocked from clearly identifying. And within a day of that discovery, he'd found his path to it — Noel Duverje.

17.

THE BATTLE

"What you are saying is impossible, Ethan? I have spent time around Patrick McClure. Granted, my feelings about him are conflicted, but if there was something monstrous possessing him, I would know it."

He shook his head and paced the den. The pieces were falling into place. Twice in the more recent past, he'd crossed paths with who he believed was Claude Barraud, always with a different face and different body, once in Paris and once in Canada. He'd always believed it was some sort of possession, but now he understood. If the body had already been abandoned, then Claude acted like some sort of skinless sea creature inhabiting someone's abandoned house. "As I said, Josephine, I don't believe any of you have ever met the real Patrick McClure. He was long gone. It was always Claude, evidently, quite adept at pretending to be something he is not."

"Oh God, but Noel, all this time has been —"

"Yes, involved with him, intimately involved with him. Not knowing who she was dealing with but being manipulated."

"What does he want from her?"

He breathed deeply. "Where is she now?"

"She was going to work at the museum."

He looked at her strangely. It really couldn't be that simple. Could it?

CB

They were on the third floor again. "Patrick, please, I really don't want to be here."

She felt as though it was freezing up, though it shouldn't be. It should be the same temperature as the rest of the building, but here, there was a pervasive draft. He'd led her out of the hallway into the Central American exhibit, and again her head swirled — too many energies. "I don't think I can stay here," she said, but he'd walked away from her, not listening. She remembered the other, Claude Barraud, had been standing nearly the same place as Patrick, pressuring her for something.

Her fiancé turned around slowly. His dark eyes were on her, but they weren't comforting. They were hard. "Now you need to pull yourself together, Noel, and try. We have our whole lives ahead of us, but we just need to get this out of the way."

Her eyes widened, completely confused. "Get what out of the way?"

He smiled at her, but it did not touch his eyes at all. "We need to give this man what he wants. Then he'll leave you alone, leave us alone."

Her heart had picked up its beat, a beat of fear. "What are you talking about?"

"He's approached me as well, Noel, Claude Barraud. He's powerful. He could destroy everything for us."

She shook her head in complete disbelief. This couldn't possibly be happening. "No, no, we can't help him."

He walked toward her, grasping her arms in his hands a little too tightly, almost painfully. "No, you're wrong, Noel. Just help him find what he's after, and he'll go. That's all we have to do."

The impact hit her like nausea. This couldn't be real. All she'd planned was crumbling before her eyes. "I need to talk to someone."

The grip tightened. "Noel, do as I ask. There isn't much time."

"Patrick?"

And then his eyes, his eyes were boring into hers. But now they weren't brown. They were green, pale icy green. "My God," she gasped. "What has he done to you?"

"Stupid girl," he rasped, shaking her. "Help me find it, and I'll release your lover."

Terror, stark and cold, swept through her. "Oh, God."

"Now," he commanded.

Shaking and with tears rolling down her face, she closed her eyes and opened to the vibrations around her.

ଓ

Ethan's heart sank as he and Josephine Duverje approached the New Orleans Museum of Art. Already there were several police cars parked beneath the front steps. Once he'd parked, Josephine shot out of the SUV without hesitation and practically flew into the front doors, where a police officer immediately stopped her.

"Please, please," she sobbed. "My daughter is in there." Just behind her, Ethan spied Noel sitting on the steps deeper in the central showroom, being questioned by an officer. Once waved on, Josephine was instantly by her side. "Noel, my God, are you all right?"

Ethan approached more slowly, noting her ashen, pale face. She glanced up at her mother and then at Ethan directly. He felt a bit of a chill at the contact. Something calamitous had occurred. "It was Patrick," she spoke flatly. "He took something from the museum and then shot a security guard as he left. He's dead."

ℭ

Noel sat quietly on the couch in Ethan's den. Ethan had suggested it, more than concerned that Claude or, rather, Patrick might turn up at Noel's apartment or even her mother's house. It bothered him immensely the girl's demeanor since the episode at the museum. But Patrick McClure was wanted now by the police for murder, and Noel — Noel seemed oddly transformed.

Josephine stood beside her, lightly patting her hand. "You might need to rest, dear. It's been so much." But her daughter didn't respond at all. Just remained silent as if in a trance.

"Josephine, I wonder if I might have a moment with Noel," he asked.

Noel's mother looked a bit shocked at his request. Clearly, it came unexpectedly. "I don't think she's up to that—"

"It's all right," Noel spoke quietly.

Josephine looked at her daughter with surprise. "Are you sure?" There was a tremor in her voice. Ethan knew that she sensed it too, that elusive but disturbing change in Noel.

"Yes, it's all right." Again, she murmured in that modulated tone with no emotion.

Josephine stood up, nervously straightening the long purple caftan blouse she wore. "All right, I can call Noel's sisters to let them know what is happening."

Ethan watched her leave, then focused his attention completely on Noel. She wasn't looking at him at all, just staring forward blankly. He settled in his chair across from the sofa, trying to understand in some respect what was happening with her. "I'm sorry, Noel," he began. "I'm sorry I didn't catch onto what he was up to earlier."

Her eyes came from some distant place and focused directly on him. "He was Patrick."

He nodded slowly, "Yes, it seems the whole time. He'd taken the body of Patrick McClure and was using it. Whoever Patrick was had left long before you knew him."

Her eyes stared at him wide, almost unseeing. "Yes, I can see that now. It was a lie, an elaborate lie."

"It seems Claude needed something."

"Something on the third floor."

"Yes, Noel, the tablet that was taken."

"The Mayan tablet," she spoke softly. "It was very powerful. I could see the hearts placed on it after sacrifices, still beating, very powerful."

"Is that what Claude wanted?" he asked her pointedly.

Her eyes seemed to focus a bit. "He wanted me to find something for him, something that would enable him to anchor to the physical plane indefinitely — something powerful."

"And that was the tablet?"

Finally, he could feel her coming back a bit, feel the familiar texture of her soul.

She shook her head, "No, it was not the tablet he needed. But I told him it was."

Ethan felt something odd, a strange sort of darkness emanate from Noel that he didn't remember feeling before. She'd turned a corner, a dark corner. "The tablet will damage him. When he tries to use the energy, it will damage him greatly."

He was surprised and torn at the same moment. How exactly, amid everything, had she managed to pull off this deception? "Noel, you've put yourself in terrible danger by doing this. He will seek you out."

It was true. She was different, changed, and it wasn't a change that he felt was at all a positive one. "Maybe," was her reply.

"What was he looking for, Noel? Do you know?"

And then she smiled a bit, "I did know. But I buried it deep within me, so he'll never find it now."

EPILOGUE

Journeys

Some journeys end in satisfaction, in resolution, but more often, in the long thread of life that I've observed, not at all. Some are simply loose, tangled threads that continue to torment, failures that scratch ever so painfully at the conscience. That is if you have one.

Not my finest hour. Perhaps I should have left well enough alone and allowed spiritual paths to unfold as they must without my interference. Or perhaps, it was my destiny to play the part I did.

The night was bringing a full moon, and I'd decided I would go into the country and unleash the wolf. To let its mindless and instinctual heart be the balm that helps me erase my regrets.

Finis

FURTHER TALES OF ETHAN GARRAINT

Wolves

"Wolves."

His eyes widened from behind the rather well-worn spectacles that he wore precariously perched on the edge of his nose. He wasn't a young man but, in contrast, a wiry, elderly fellow who didn't much like change and even less surprises. So, in a procrastinating fashion, he removed the glasses, pulling an old handkerchief from his back pocket and leisurely wiping the lenses. Simultaneously, his still razor-sharp mind contemplated a backdoor out of this dilemma. He sighed, again positioning the glasses on the end of his nose and giving just the hint of a smile that said he was just an old fool running a curio shop in the French Quarter. Taking a deep breath that felt clearly as though it rattled deeply somewhere in the recesses of his brittle ribs, he played his best cards. "Is there something, in particular, I could help you with today?"

There was the finest flicker of a smile across a pair of young, dark red lips. The eyes in a fine-boned oval face stared back at him as though they were neatly and concisely ripping away the layers of his well-contrived façade. The eyes were green. His wife, Roberta, of nearly sixty years, had green eyes as well, but not at all like these. His wife's eyes were filled with light and color. But not these. These were dark, like a forest on the verge of night. Any light that tried to reflect was muffled out by something unseen within.

The mouth was moving, and he was watching it curiously, compelled perhaps, he thought, somewhat distantly. Was she trying to entrance him or suffocate him? At this moment, both felt like a tangible probability.

"Wolves," she murmured again. Of course, he knew of what she was speaking. He might play the fool from time to time, but he certainly wasn't one. Long ago, he was told when it was first placed in his keeping that someone would come for it one day with only that single word as their calling card. And he, out of more than obligation — out of a binding indisputable agreement — must surrender it. Of course, at the time, he was well-paid. In fact, he had never been better paid for any single acquisition in all his years. But it was so long ago, thirty, perhaps closer to forty years back. And that payment was just a distant, fleeting memory now. While the object itself, well, it was worth an untold fortune.

Abruptly interrupting the meandering of his mind, he felt a slim hand come to rest on his. His eyes looked down. They were long slender fingers, flesh that was paler than warmed by the sun. But then, the delicate hand began to squeeze with a strength he did not understand. "I don't have time for this old man. Give it to me," she rasped. Those lightless eyes were wide now and so very frightening to him.

"Give you what?" He choked out. But it was his final lie. For in his mind, as clear as though he were seeing it before him, his building, his store of so many years, and he within were engulfed in flames. It must be happening now, at the moment, for the flames were wildly everywhere, burning him, scorching the flesh on his arms, until he could see the white of his very own skeleton. "Uoohh!" he gasped, the unintelligible and desperate words of a dying man.

And then, clearly, sharply penetrating into the horror of his own hell, he heard a voice, a voice speaking to him within his own mind. "Now let's try this again," she whispered because there was no need to shout. She had won. "Wolves," this time it rolled off her tongue like the sweetest poetry.

℠

"This is foolishness, pure foolishness, my dear."

She grimaced, "So you've said." She perched the cell phone a bit unstably on her shoulder and checked the rear-view mirror. What was foolish was taking a call on an unfamiliar highway while she was driving an unfamiliar rental car.

"Where are you now?"

"I'm driving." Luckily, it was a clear stretch — this last piece of the journey between New Orleans and the small south-central city that was her destination.

"You're not going to tell me, are you?"

"It's best not. I'll fill you in when everything is done."

"And you, my little sister, will you be done too?"

She sighed deeply. How she loved her older Brother, and his protectiveness. Ostensibly, he was the only family she had now, except for certain unknown factions. But just now, his protectiveness felt more than a bit smothering. "Well, let's hope not."

"Are you sure you're reading that thing right? What if you end up with the wrong one?"

"Charles, you have to have a little faith. I am not without my own gifts."

"Cecile, I don't want to lose you."

"I know. Just have a little trust in me."

∞

On the way into town, she picked up a street map so she wouldn't be entirely clueless as to where she was going. And then, just off the highway, she checked into a motel. It was one of a moderately priced chain. She'd stayed in better. She could most certainly afford better. She and her Brother had money. Her parents had left them well off, well, when they died. But just now, the surroundings didn't matter much. She only needed a place to regroup.

Cecile placed her small suitcase on the bed and sat quietly beside it, contemplative. What she'd done to the old man in the antique shop had been cruel and unfair. And certainly, on some level, she was ashamed. But she'd sensed his greed, his reluctance to relinquish it, the thing she needed.

Steadying her nerves, she reached into her black leather purse and drew out the bundle of material that she'd wrapped it in. It was a fine white, raw silk piece of fabric. Rather gingerly, she laid it on the bed and began to unwrap its folds. Already her fingertips quivered from the emanations of power, although she had not even touched it. It sat in its mahogany box latched with a clasp of pure silver. It was quite valuable, perhaps priceless in its construction, certainly in its origin. It was understandable that the old man did not want to part with it.

She rubbed the palms of her hand together briskly, trying to drive away the chill that had settled in her fingers. She had spent enough years studying the magical arts to know that handling such powerfully enchanted tools did come with a price. Taking a nearly painful breath, she quickly flipped the latch, opening the box of the Houdin Trouveur.

That it was stunning was undeniable — beautiful, quite ornate, constructed purely of platinum and black onyx. The platinum arms of the antiquated compass fluttered momentarily and then swirled in a deliberate direction, markedly toward the southeast. She sighed. He would be there. The murderer of her parents was somewhere in this city.

CB

Something was off. He'd felt it all day, deep down in his skin, actually the night before as well. And irritatingly, the dreams had come, a sweep of redness and then fire, fire exploding pure and white. What it all meant, he wasn't so sure. He'd given up this divination business, this reading of dreams, some time ago — in fact, two hundred years ago, to be exact. For some time, with the exception of a few minor lapses, life had become quite placid for Ethan Garraint. That was the name he'd adopted several decades earlier. And he had to admit he'd grown fond of it. This part of the country was quite welcoming to those of a French descent.

Ethan continued to polish a heavy, black oak wardrobe mirror that he'd just put the finishing touches on for the festival today. He enjoyed working with black oak. There was something depthless about its sheen. But then again, black oak, pine, maple, and cherry wood all had their respective charms. For a moment, he glanced at the reflection serenely staring back at him from the long oval mirror. From his appearance, he could not be mistaken for a man of more than thirty. His light blue-grey eyes and thick blonde hair suggested an almost innocent quality that his soul disagreed with. He'd been alive too long and seen too much to be naïve about much of anything.

He finished polishing the wood of the mirror, more interested in his creation than anything else. He'd found some solace through the long years and endless solitude in developing this craft. There was a strange contentment he'd found in working with the wood that eased the burdens that his unusual life had deemed he should carry. In some ways, he felt as though he imbued his creations with small pieces of his soul. After all, even he couldn't live forever, not with so many people trying to kill him.

03

"How will you be able to find him with it? Doesn't it just seek out any werewolf?" Charles had asked her this, among other questions, before she'd set out from Boston nearly five days ago.

"Well, I haven't spent all these years studying and developing my gifts without the intent of making use of them. As an insurance policy, I will work an incantation that will affix the Houdin Trouveur solely toward him, toward our parent's killer."

He'd stared at her with great anxiety within his acute, dark eyes. "I don't like it. And regardless of your intentions, I don't think our parents would like it either."

She frowned explicitly, "Well, they're not here to give us an opinion, are they?"

He looked away, clearly disturbed by her words. "I know they would want you to get on with your life Cecile, not become obsessed with vengeance."

She sighed. They'd had this discussion before countless times. But evidently, Charles felt it worthwhile to try one last attempt to dissuade her. "They weren't the type to look the other way. They wouldn't have allowed an injustice to stand. You knew them. You were older when they died."

His eyes flickered gently across her face. He was a strong man, a stern man, except when it came to his younger sister. He had always reserved his kinder nature for his dealings with her. "They had limits, Cecile. They were human. I know they wouldn't have approved of how deeply you've gone into these dark arts."

She hardened herself. Now was not the time to be thrown off course. Not when she was so close. "I've only done what was necessary. I can't go after Le Guerrier unprotected."

He smiled grimly, "Don't call him that. It makes him sound too much like a mythology. No, I know you feel you've done what you've had to. But at what cost, Cecile?"

She blocked his words from her mind. She couldn't afford to question herself now, not now. "It's time, Charles. Did you get me what I need?"

"Yes," he said quietly, seemingly resigned for the moment. "The location of the seeker."

She'd smiled broadly. If he was nothing else, Charles Bissett was thorough. "And the password to get it?"

"Yes, my dear one, all of that. But finding the monster won't kill him for you."

She so wished he was not so anxious. If anyone should be, it should be her. But an odd sort of serenity had settled within her. Perhaps, it was the acknowledgment of what she must do — her acceptance of what her long years of aimlessness and restlessness had brought her to. "I know that. I've spent years tracking Le Guerrier. I've researched, learned every scrap, every nuance that is knowable about him."

"But these last fifteen years, he's completely fallen off the radar. Even with my extensive connections, no one knows anything. How do you even know he's alive?"

"I know it." She stated flatly with complete conviction. "I would know if he were dead."

He straightened up in the brown leather chair by the fireplace in their study. At that moment, it struck her quite poignantly. She remembered the nights she'd curled up in it as a little girl when her nightmares kept her from sleep and wondered in a fleeting twist of yearning if she would ever see it or her Brother again. "How would you know it, Cecile?" he asked.

A simple question with such a complicated answer, "Because I would feel peace if he were dead." There was a look in his eyes at this — perhaps sadness, perhaps disbelief. "Don't worry, Charles," she murmured.

"I can't help it. I don't want to lose you too."

"I can beat him. I know him completely."

And then he smiled grimly, "But what if he's changed?"

Cஐ

She'd packed the tiny pistol deep within her purse. It was loaded with three silver bullets that Charles had managed to get blessed by a Bishop in Northern Massachusetts. Anyone else making such a request would probably be tossed out unceremoniously on their backside but not Charles. Charles was a rich man, and money and donations often made the ridiculous acceptable.

Late the previous night, Cecile had performed an intricate locator spell on the Houdin Trouveur. It had enabled her to gain a more precise fix on his location. But as a consequence, it drained her terribly. It seemed the magical compass had to pull in a great deal of energy from its user to fulfill its purpose. She hadn't anticipated the severity of this complication. It was clear she should use the Trouveur as seldom as possible lest she lose too much of her power. She slept deeply that night and dreamed of crowds of people laughing and dancing and colorful booths and exhibits all about her. Then she saw fire, white blinding fire, somewhere else.

When she ventured into the lobby that morning for coffee, she noticed the signs hanging up promoting the festival. It was then she made the connection. Clearly, these were the images from the night before. Donning blue jeans, a white cotton shirt, and a pair of lace-up, black leather boots that she'd bought on a trip to France the year before, Cecile then obtained directions to the festivities, which oddly turned out to be exactly southeast of her location. Everything was falling into place, and that, more than anything, made her extremely uneasy.

ଔ

Amelia Gerard had just turned twenty and was majoring in communications at the local university. As the crowds milled around her on this bright Saturday in October, she felt annoyed and a bit preoccupied. She'd left behind a group of friends near the stage, listening to one of the musical acts booked for the festival. She'd told them she was going for another beer, but instead, she bypassed the refreshment stands and wandered most deliberately into the artisan section.

Although there was quite a mixing of people and more than a little stirring of dust from the ground, she was able to locate the man she sought quite readily. She stood beside the booth where he'd set up his collection of furniture pieces for the occasion. She waited quietly but not entirely patiently as he finished talking to what she surmised was a potential customer. It was some minutes before he noticed her, but he did greet her with a welcoming smile that, at that moment, felt well worth the wait. "Ms. Gerard."

"Mr. Garraint," she responded lightly.

He wore a dark T-shirt with khaki pants that she thought made him look particularly handsome, but then again, she was utterly smitten with the man. "So, are you enjoying the festival on this fine day?" He asked with his fluid drawl that she had never quite been able to identify. It wasn't exactly local, but, in some ways, it did seem a bit French.

She tipped her head a bit, warming under his gaze, "Well, it's a bit crowded and a bit loud. But other than that, I'd have to say yes."

He moved a rocking chair he'd been showing to someone further back into the open booth as he spoke to her. It felt odd to think that she'd only met him only a few months earlier. Then she'd been involved in a project for a journalism class, interviewing local artists.

Initially, perhaps to her ignorance, she hadn't considered furniture making an art. But once she met Ethan Garraint, she was enlightened, and that opinion was radically revised. Intriguing truly seemed too ineffectual a word to describe him. There was an aura about him, a subtle but powerfully enigmatic aura that captivated her. She was quite sure he was a good ten years her senior, but that hadn't stopped her from forming a romantic interest. After all, she always considered herself quite mature for her age.

He nodded, "It is busy today. But that's good for everyone's business."

His eyes had flickered over her only briefly and then continued to glance around the crowds as though he was watching for something.

"Is everything all right, Ethan?" She asked, wondering why she was not holding his attention today.

He glanced up at her, looking a bit pensive, then smiling. "You should go find your friends Amelia and enjoy yourself. I'm afraid I'll be quite busy with things here today."

Her eyes widened, and then he nodded, reaffirming his previous declaration. She was being dismissed, and it chaffed, particularly his abruptness. But she did have to admit. There was something else in his voice that was quite grave, that told her that this was for her own good. Although why, she couldn't quite put her finger on. "All right then, have a good day." She murmured reluctantly.

"Yes, yes, and you as well."

ᑋ

From some yards away, Cecile watched. It must be him, but she couldn't be positive and certainly couldn't confront him in the middle of such a crowd. Werewolf or not, she would be arrested for shooting an unarmed man. The only way to be positive was to use the Trouveur. But that, too, was risky. It was too powerful to go unnoticed by such an ancient magical being. In addition, it would tip her hand and, in all probability, leave her to the same fate as her parents.

Her eyes locked on and carefully followed the young blond he'd been speaking to.

With great focus, she sent out an impulse that encouraged her to pass near Cecile. As she did, Cecile propelled a discreet energy marker toward her that landed on the woman's arm. With this in place, she could be easily traced when Cecile required her.

ᑋ

Amelia left the fairgrounds around five. Her friends intended to stay much later and move on to some downtown clubs as the evening progressed, but a strange fatigue and melancholy had seized her. She knew she was being silly. There was nothing between her and Ethan Garraint, nothing but her own fantasies. The man had always been kind, cordial, and charming in a way that some might construe as flirtatious, but then again, it could just be his manner.

She flung open the door to her dorm room, shutting it loudly behind her, and flopped vigorously onto the bed. If she was anything, she was practical and knew when to cut her losses. Tomorrow she would remove Mr. Garraint from her consciousness and her radar. Then she would look around to find other, more attainable fish in the sea. She closed her eyes, allowing her excessive tiredness to take hold. It could have been moments, or even hours later, when she awoke to a very quiet knock on her door. Amelia glanced at the clock by her bed. It was six-thirty. Sara, her roommate, wasn't due back for some time yet.

Slowly sitting up, she was feeling a bit disoriented. But again, merely seconds later, another light tap on the door. "Just a minute," she called out, her voice still croaky from sleep.

She rose on shaky feet, trying to smooth out her long blonde hair as she approached the door. She wondered with distraction if she was getting sick because the room actually felt as though it was swirling around her. Her trembling hand touched the knob of the door. It felt cold and moist beneath her fingertips. But then maybe it was her. Her hands did feel strangely clammy right now.

Just before she turned the knob, it occurred to her, like a flash through her mind, that she shouldn't. But her pragmatic sense pushed that impulse aside as she opened the door. In that instant, time seemed to rush around her in a blur as an impossibly strong hand reached out and grabbed her by the throat.

☙

Ethan began to close up his booth somewhere around seven in the evening. Others set up near him had left earlier, but he waited as long as he could. He was expecting something. He was no clairvoyant, but he did have very acute feelings and a sense of things. Today, he sensed a menace about. And more to the point, he smelled it. There was dark magic in the air.

So, he waited and watched all day. But this menace was a clever one and remained hidden. This, however, did not overly concern him. One thing he did have that all these extraordinarily young souls milling about him seemed to lack was patience, infinite, inexhaustible patience. He could wait it out.

As he loaded his small van with the pieces of furniture that did not sell at the fair, he heard from quite a distance the footsteps approaching the truck. His powerful sense of smell identified their author rather quickly. He smiled to himself even before she reached him.

Persistent was a word that seemed appropriate.

He allowed her to approach without turning around as he finished packing the van. This type of complication he felt quite sure he could manage with very little peril to himself.

"Ethan," she whispered.

And then he turned around with a smile. "Amelia, this is a very isolated place now for you to be all alone."

She did not smile back at him in her usual, coquettish manner. "I'm not alone. You're here. Aren't you concerned about it being so isolated?"

He sighed. She was in a somber mood tonight. Not her ordinarily light-hearted self. "I am not a beautiful young woman, and I can handle myself." He frowned, "What's the matter, little one? You seem very grim tonight."

She tilted her head, and those lovely blue eyes looked at him oddly in the semi-darkness. "I need to talk to you, Ethan, about something very serious. Can we go somewhere private?"

He grinned a bit, trying to put her more at ease. "Now, that might ruin your reputation."

But he was a bit surprised. It did nothing to thaw the gravity of her demeanor. "It's important, please."

"I was headed back to the store to bring the furniture."

"Could we go there and talk?" Her voice sounded nearly pleading, but it didn't reach the eyes. They remained distant. Something was definitely amiss. It seemed clear to him now that it was best to discover what all this was about.

"Where is your car?"

She shook her head, soft blond hair whipping about her shoulders. "A friend dropped me."

He nodded, "Fine, then let's go."

She said nothing but quietly climbed into the van's front seat beside him.

⊂Ӡ

It becomes quite odd when a scenario you've built up in your mind since you were a child finally comes to fruition. Every nuance is painstakingly planned, pulled somewhere from an endless well of grief, then later disappointment, and nursed to an excruciatingly fine point of razor-sharp detail.

She had rehearsed the scene all her life, put endless preparations into the part, and lived and breathed for just these few paltry moments. And nothing, absolutely nothing, was as she expected.

Cecile retreated into some quiet place, where the observer watches and marvels at the contradictions that reality unravels. The man next to her was charming and warm — not cold and brittle like the killer of her dreams but something else entirely. As they walked into the dimly lit front room of his St. Julien Street establishment, his calm, soothing demeanor sickened her. It twisted at her like a poorly placed knife, lodged somewhere precariously between her ribs, making breathing a bit difficult.

As she crossed the threshold, a sudden blurriness swept up in front of her eyes. She forced her mind to concentrate and funnel even more energy into her façade, although she knew it was ill-advised. Taking on the form of another visage was a gamble, risky, stretching well beyond her limitations. It couldn't go on for long. Besides, it was best to finish him off before he was onto her. Best to be done with it. But the idea of just killing him now and leaving felt oddly empty. She needed more to put this all at rest. She needed —

He grabbed her arm to steady her. "Are you all right, Amelia?"

She nodded and murmured. "Yes, just feeling a little weak. I haven't eaten." She tried to avoid his eyes. She had read an account once from a seventeenth-century monk chronicling the history of Northern Gaul. It was a local uprising, in some obscure way involving Le Guerrir. The monk referred quite pointedly to the hypnotic quality of the foreigner's eyes. She remembered it now, thinking it strange at the time. After all, wasn't it vampires, not werewolves, who held the hypnotic gaze? Then again, he had lived an abnormally long time and had no doubt picked up a few interesting tricks along the way.

She felt his hand gently grasp her chin, deliberately tilting her head to face him. She had no choice. Her pistol was in her purse, not exactly accessible right at this moment. She allowed her gaze to meet his, concentrating heavily on the incantation that separated her from disaster.

127

The light was dim, but at this moment, his eyes appeared markedly darker than she remembered at the festival grounds. They were blue but also grey, not a light grey but a dark, turbulent one. He was looking for something. He felt the difference. She was sure of it but hopefully hadn't fleshed it out yet. "Tell me what's really wrong," he murmured.

Her heart was beating wildly with fear. She dug, dug deep into the flashes she'd picked up out of Amelia Gerard's mind even as she ravaged and drained her life's energy earlier this evening. Then she hadn't thought about how ruthless she'd been, and now there was no time to reflect on such collateral damages. Desperate, she hooked onto something — her unrequited affection for this man. It was just enough to throw him temporarily off-balance. With deliberation, she put her arms around his neck, reaching up and giving him the most passionate kiss she could muster.

At first, she felt him freeze in total surprise. Good, that's exactly what she wanted. Keep him surprised and off-balance. And then, startlingly, he pulled her closer against him and returned the kiss with a fervor that she found completely unexpected. She expected a rejection, not capitulation.

In reflex, forgetting where she was and the goal, Cecile abruptly tore herself out of the embrace. "What are you doing?" she spat out without thinking.

He stood there staring at her, and then his face broke out in a smile she could only describe as quite engaging. "I was kissing you back, my dear. You know, you really should decide what you want."

She quickly regrouped, coming back with the most insipidly, vulnerable expression she could concoct. "I want you to stop toying with me, Ethan. I want to mean something to you, not be a passing fancy."

The smile drifted away from his mouth, and a grimmer expression replaced it. "Perhaps, we should sit down and talk this out, Amelia. He motioned to a small cherry wood dinette at the back of the shop. "Why don't you sit down, and I'll make us a cup of tea." She nodded, still trying to look the part of a confused, lovesick female. She clutched her purse close to her side and slowly sat at the table.

Softly, he patted her back and whispered in her ear, "Be back in just a minute." And then he disappeared into a back room. She looked down. Her eyes were blurring again, twenty minutes to half an hour. That was the very longest she could retain the appearance of Amelia Gerard. Her hand reached down into her purse and fingered the pistol, but the back of it brushed against the cloth that held the Trouveur. Even through the material, it burned against her hand.

She was sure it was him. It must be. But she would like to confirm it before she took his life. This much she owed to her parents, to be absolutely sure. She grasped the Trouveur and placed it on the table.

03

He had a small kitchen in one of the back rooms of his shop. It was a galley across from the larger studio where he did much of his woodwork. There was an old-fashioned kettle that he was using to heat the water for their tea. Of course, the microwave would be much faster, but he wanted to take the extra minutes to contemplate. It seemed as though all the hairs on the back of his neck were standing on end, alerted in nearly a violent fashion to a danger in his proximity.

But all that was present was Amelia — beautiful, unpredictable, and dare he say unstable Amelia. He placed the teabags into the two mugs as the copper kettle rattled on the stove. He enjoyed the simplicity of his life these days, minus all the trappings that people become so intertwined with that they can no longer see the truth.

He took the kettle off the stove, poured the steaming water into the cups, and watched quietly as they steeped. In a life stripped of those things that separate one from clear vision, it is easier to discriminate truth from illusions.

The things he'd felt essentially about Amelia were oddly distorted tonight. She was not a person to behave erratically. She was conservative, practical and would not gamble unless it was warranted. But tonight, he swirled one of the tea bags in hot water until it bled its color throughout, did not add up. He didn't smell alcohol. He didn't detect drug use, and for her, that, too, would have been entirely out of character.

He turned toward the front room, reacting to something, something subtle — a sort of crackle in the air. And then suddenly, directly in his heart area, he felt a pressure so acute that he flinched at its impact.

What he did next was foolish, but he had come to live a simple, uncomplicated life as much out of the shadows as was possible for a creature like him. So, he walked, without caution, quickly into the front room.

The table where he'd left her was unoccupied, but even from across the room, he could see a nearly luminescent object sitting on top of it. The gentle pressure in his heart only intensified as he approached, but nothing could quell his curiosity. It was perhaps a yard away from it that he stopped, his curiosity quite satisfied as he clearly identified what he was looking at. One piece to an irritating puzzle had fallen into place. "That bastard Houdin," he muttered with part contempt and part amusement. "He swore he'd destroyed the damn thing."

And then, from behind a large cypress armoire, a rather shadowy figure emerged. Her voice was not mellow and fluid like Amelia's but instead deep and raspy "Too bad for you that he didn't."

His eyes first took in the tiny pistol pointed at him and, second, the features of the woman that held it. The hair was long, thick, and auburn, and the eyes, as far as he could perceive a dark mossy green shade. At this, the rest of the puzzle fell into place, for the resemblance was unmistakable. He smiled broadly, never one to face his demise without a light heart. "Well, if I'm not mistaken, you must be Cecile. I've made it my business to keep track of the Bissett children." She frowned. Evidently, that wasn't the reaction she'd been expecting. "I knew your mother. She was a resourceful woman but evidently not as resourceful as you are."

Her voice was quiet and steely, "I'm here to kill you."

He nodded, "So I see, but not before we have a nice visit, I hope. After all, I'm the only one who can tell you the truth about your parents' death."

ೞ

The noise in her head roared around her in the room, but he clearly didn't hear it. She steadied herself, although her knees shook with weakness. With extreme concentration, she gripped the pistol, although her hands were so chilled that she could scarcely feel herself holding it.

She could see Charles in her mind as clearly as if he stood before her. "At what cost, Cecile, revenge at what cost?"

Her vision was blotchy, and parts of the room completely blotted out. When she'd used the Trouveur, it had been different. It glowed and shook, and the pointer spun toward the back room. But before it was finished, she'd felt it emanate something, a force that had been subtle before. It pulled energy from her as

131

if tearing it directly out of her heart. But she couldn't let him see. She only had to finish it. That was all that mattered.

"I'm not a fool Le Guerrier. Do you really think I've come here for a chat?"

He moved slightly, but she wasn't sure. Her vision was so bad now. Everything was indistinct light and shadows. "Your mother was a very determined woman. I think finishing me off might have been a feather in her cap. But your father, I don't think he cared much, except for her. She was everything to him."

He'd moved now. She was sure. "Stay still, or I'll end all of this now."

The movement stopped. The only way she could see him was reflected in the light. Was this what it was like going blind? She followed the impressions that were left in her vision. "It was in Italy, you know. I don't like to travel much now, but I did that year. They didn't know it, but I came there to learn from a master furniture maker. Isn't that amusing? The werewolf hunted down because he wanted to make furniture better?"

She breathed deeply, raggedly. She could see her parents in her mind, and then Charles and Amelia. She'd left her on the dorm room floor, not dead, but close to it. "Stop talking," she rasped.

"You know, they thought it would be safe that night. It wasn't a full moon. It would be an easy kill for them, they thought. But the wolf came out that night."

There was deep, ravaging, painful breaths now. "What do you mean?"

She looked around the room, but she'd lost sight of him. He wasn't moving, just hidden in the shadows. "I learned how to control the wolf, summon it at will without the necessity of a full moon. An old magician helped me perfect the technique." She focused on the direction of his voice, but it seemed to be coming from everywhere. "His name was Houdin."

It seemed moments before the reality rolled over her. "What, what did you say?"

"A 19th-century magician, cantankerous fellow, but loyal and brilliant. Haven't you figured it out yet, Cecile?"

"What?" she murmured. She couldn't feel her hands at all. They were like ice, as was her skin, as was her mind.

"That thing, the Trouveur you've been using, has been killing you, feeding a poisonous fire into your veins."

"That's impossible," she barely could get the words out. He was standing next to her, but she couldn't stop him. She couldn't feel the gun. It might have dropped. She didn't know.

"The Trouveur kills the person who uses it. Slowly, I grant you, but my friend was a merciless bastard."

She slipped to her knees, seeing Charles taking her out of the chair in the study when she was a little girl, whispering away the nightmares. She barely heard his voice. "He was merciless. But I am not." She heard the low growl beside her but did not see the wolf. She'd already walked into the white fire.

ༀ

Two days later, Amelia Gerard woke up in the hospital. Her mother was sitting beside her, holding her hand. Tears were running down her face as Amelia first opened her eyes. Two days after that, an arrangement of yellow roses arrived with a card that read, *Best Wishes on a Speedy Recovery, All My Regards, Ethan.* That was the last time she ever heard from him.

THE BROKEN WINDOW

"I'm not sure, not at all sure what the problem is."

"Is it the glass?"

"Doesn't seem to be. It's made of the same glass as all the other windows along the wall."

"Perhaps the sizing of the glass is off."

"I don't know. That seems to be a bit unlikely. After all, this is the third time."

"Are you serious? The third time?"

"Yes, Ma'am, last Thursday, Tuesday, and then today."

Moira frowned. It was Saturday evening at the East Bank Regional Public Library, and she was staring at a two-story tall wall of plate glass windows — in particular, one pane whose glass was not shattered but oddly cracked from the center out.

"You want me to put up the yellow tape?"

She shrugged with distraction. "I suppose. I'll call someone to fix it, but it's the weekend. They probably won't do anything until Monday." She stared for a moment, oddly transfixed for some inexplicable reason. After all, it was just a window. It didn't mean anything.

Moira was a part-time librarian at the library, at least for present. Her plans were uncertain, her life in a flux. She didn't intend to make a career here, just fill a gap or a chasm, as she often looked at it. She'd actually only been working here a month, and the window problem. Well, the night security guards indicated it started about two weeks ago. She tapped her pen on the wooden counter in front of her — just two weeks.

"Working late tonight, Moira?"

She glanced up from the computer terminal from which she'd been working on an inventory. "Yes, until nine. How about you?"

Sally Clark stared at her with that wild animated look that she always seemed to possess. "No, no, I'm out of here at six. Wish you were coming. My boyfriend has a friend — "

Her voice droned on in Moira's ears, but she had tuned her out. Sally was, well, predictable. She was closing in on forty, and although Moira was only several years her junior, she looked on in trepidation with anyone Sally could set her up with. Sally was a nice woman, but Moira was sure their taste in men might not even rub elbows in this universe.

She snapped a book closed, looking up at Sally, whose hair had evidently been dyed an odd reddish-blonde color when Moira wasn't paying attention. But it seemed as if she'd concluded her ramble. "You have a great evening."

"Maybe some other time," Sally tacked on enthusiastically. She was actually a nice lady, and Moira should be nicer. But, well, she wasn't. So instead of responding, she just smiled, waiting patiently for her co-worker to make an exit.

It was Saturday evening, but the staff in the whole two-story structure of the East Bank library would be there tonight; however, there were only four instead of the usual six closing.

The desk in reference where she stood had a clear view of that problematic cracked window. It was odd, unnerving, and alerted her to something deep within her skin — something that perhaps told her it was time to move on, although she'd only been here a mere month.

She sighed deeply from somewhere at her core, glancing down at her hands on the wooden counter. And right on the ring finger was a tell-tale white mark indicating where a band had once been, a band that was now missing.

Instinctively, she balled her left hand up in a fist almost protectively.

She ran her hand through her short brown hair. It was a sensible haircut she'd gotten just before she came here. After all, if Moira Archer wanted to be a librarian, she needed to look the part. But she missed her hair, her long auburn-colored hair that she'd dyed a shade of dark brown. It was best not to stand out. Nervously, she strummed her fingers again on the counter, staring at the broken window, broken strangely, almost as if it imploded internally from pressure but pressure from an odd point.

She breathed in deeply. It was unfortunate because she'd hoped to stay longer. It was unfortunate but unavoidable. Tonight, after work, she would go home to her small apartment on West Napoleon Avenue, pack up her car, and leave — leave behind the furniture that she'd just bought and decorated with, leave behind the friends, although just a handful that she'd just begun to make, leave behind everything and start over somewhere else. She thought perhaps of the mountains, maybe driving up into the Ozarks. There it would be more difficult. There were so many varying energies that would block things. But then again, that was why she'd come to New Orleans with the same thought, perhaps if she'd settled deeper in the city.

But she shook these second guesses out of her mind. The broken window could be a coincidence, but she was not in a position to gamble.

She tried to focus on the screen in front of her. It was just after six. She just needed to get through the next three hours, although she was not beyond just walking out. That, indeed, was a possibility.

Again, she stared at the computer screen before her, mind cluttered, unable to concentrate. It really wasn't as if it mattered if she worked much tonight. She'd already decided she was leaving. And the fatality of that understanding left her with a heavy heart. She liked her little apartment with its light wicker furniture and the pretty floral pictures she'd hung on its walls. It felt like life.

She shook her head a bit and headed to a shelving cart by the side of the desk. This she could do right now. It required little brain power.

α

The long aisles of the library were narrow and smelled musty to him — but then again, his sense of smell was of the acutest kind, which was a blessing and a curse. Of course, he thought with little humor, that seemed to be the theme of his life.

Ethan wore a long trench coat that he was of half a mind to divest himself of. After all, he had spent enough time over the centuries in Southern Louisiana to be aware of its humid climate. It was only two days until Halloween, late October, and still summer as far as this area of North America was concerned. But he was on a mission, a delicate mission, and so, as his indulgent nature demanded, he had wanted to dress the part.

Then again, he was also suffocating, so in expediency, Ethan pulled off the trench coat and flipped it over his arm shaking out his longish blonde hair. He checked his watch — eight o'clock. Well, that gave him about an hour to exercise his diplomatic powers. Lucky for him, there would be no full moon this Hallow's Eve. A full moon on that particular night or in the days leading up to it could be particularly, well in his case, unraveling.

He took in a deep whiff of the musty air around him, trying to focus beyond the well-worn stench of book covers that had been untouched for far too long.

No, it was beyond the human occupants of this building where he focused, well beyond.

A slight smile crossed his lips. Yes, he had marked her.

 og

Moira was trying to relax, but her skin prickled. For some time, the mindless shelving of books had placed her into a thoughtless reverie. But that had seemed to pass now. Something had changed. Only four were on duty tonight, but if she feigned illness, they could close up without her. She moved the cart of books she'd been pushing around all evening around the corner of a bookshelf, then stopped.

Several sections of books away down at the other end of the long stretch was a tall, blondish man dressed in black with a coat draped over his arm.

She didn't know who he was, but she could see clearly what he was — a werewolf, a werewolf standing right in the middle of the East Bank Regional Library.

Moira took a deep breath and braced herself. After all, they were in a public place, and the last she'd checked, the moon was at a very slim crescent. So, all she had to do was play dumb — just be the reclusive little librarian that she had chosen to be.

She gave the stranger a glance, a brief acknowledging smile, then turned to her task of shelving books, focusing intently. Perhaps his presence here had nothing to do with her. Perhaps it was one of those odd random coincidences that the universe seemed intent on perpetrating on ordinary folk.

Another deep breath to stabilize her, yes indeed, that was what she had chosen to be, ordinary folk — just like Sally, or dour Tom at the front desk, or combative Jessica Renard up in Special Collections. Yes, surely, all of them were extraordinary in their own unique ordinariness.

She grasped the three hardback Nora Robert's novels from the cart and placed them on the shelf. Then she froze, on the spot, still facing forward. But she could feel it all over her back, as tangible as if he'd directly placed his hands there. Of course, he hadn't. He was just standing there quietly, directly behind her.

With little choice now, she slowly turned to face him. He looked to be in his thirties, bearded with a mustache, and longish blonde hair just grazing the top of the black turtleneck he wore. And his eyes, which she was close enough to see, were an eerie blue-gray color, staring at her as though he hadn't a care in the world.

And everything, still everything about him, screamed wolf to her.

"Can I help you with something?" she asked softly.

It was odd what hit her most acutely in the next moment. A touch of compassion seemed to reach his eyes — something she found most unexpected. "I think perhaps maybe I can help you. Moira Archer, is it?"

140

It was a strange moment filled with some duality. Surely, there was the disappointment that her hopes had been crushed. Oddly enough, and there was no denying her existence had always been filled with oddities, she also felt a measure of relief.

For although she'd pegged him as a werewolf, she was also sensing no malice, no threat — quite unexpected.

C3

Ethan felt oddly frustrated as a lingering thought floated through his mind. "Why were all the good ones taken?"

There was a coffee shop or rather a small coffee bar with accompanying tables situated in the foyer of the library. He and the woman who was calling herself Moira Archer sat there; she sipped a hot mug of peppermint tea, and he, a hot coffee mocha — something that called itself coffee but tasted a bit more like hot chocolate. But given that he'd nurtured his sweet tooth through the many centuries of his existence, it suited him well.

A brief interlude having a sweet and spending time with an intriguing woman didn't seem like a bad deal for an old lycanthrope like himself.

"So," he smiled engagingly, "how do you like the city?"

She slowly placed her hot, in fact still steaming, cup of tea on the table and stared at him with eyes that were large and dark but, for some odd reason, reminded him of some strange violet tone. Of course, that couldn't be so — what human had violet-colored eyes? And then he stopped himself. Yes, what human, indeed?

"My break isn't that long Mr. — I'm sorry. What did you say your name was again?"

"Ethan Garraint."

She nodded slowly. "And may I assume you were sent here by —" she paused, so he obligingly filled in. After all, there really wasn't time to be coy. In fact, there didn't seem to be time for much of anything.

"Well, actually an old friend — your husband."

Her face showed no surprise. In fact, not much emotion of any kind. But then again, for a woman like this, it was most predictable that her husband would attempt to get her back.

"I am not wholly unacquainted with my husband's acquaintances, but I don't recall —."

"We go way back," he replied, taking a quick sip of the cocoa/coffee concoction. "Actually, early Renaissance, in Italy, we first crossed paths."

"I see," she pronounced a bit definitively. "I'll get to the point Mr. —"

"Ethan," he interrupted. He had to get this on a friendlier plateau, or it would be a wasted effort before he even began.

"Ethan, you can tell my husband that I am not —"

"Yes, yes that you are not coming back."

Now she looked at him a bit oddly. Finally, he'd said something that had elicited a reaction. "Yes, I mean, isn't that why you are here?"

He sighed deeply, trying to find the appropriate avenue to navigate around the truth. "Well, Moira, not exactly. He is concerned about you. You see, it seems your absence has created a bit of, well, imbalance."

Her brow wrinkled slightly, but it did nothing to mar her delicate loveliness. He was not at all at a loss to explain his friend's fascination, dare he say obsession, with the woman before him.

"What do you mean imbalance?"

He leaned in a bit closer to her. "Moira, haven't you felt ever since you left that you were being followed?"

A slight downturn of her finely shaped lips, "Well, yes, but I thought that was just him, well, trying to get me to come home. After all, he sent you."

"Yes, but he sent me to warn you. He hasn't been trying to get you back. Just protect you."

There was a hesitation, clearly a moment to soak in unconsidered information. "I have no idea what you're talking about, Ethan," she almost rasped out in what he unmistakably pegged as mild panic.

"Think Moira, the window. They're coming for you — the minions breaking in from their dimension to disrupt the order of things."

Again, she stared at him with violet-colored eyes. Perhaps they were violet, and with indulgence, he thought perhaps he was the only one who could see that.

She leaned back in her chair, contemplating, he thought, sipping her tea. "What are you trying to say — that to restore the natural order of things, I have to return?"

He shrugged a bit. Who was he to get in the middle of another's marital discord? He'd tried it himself once so long ago and found not only was it impractical for a werewolf, but he himself didn't prove to be exactly the best marital material. "I don't know if it's that simple, Moira. It has more to do with discord, ill-feelings. If you both could come to an understanding, it might stabilize things."

And then the unexpected happened. Her wide violet-colored eyes seemed to tear up as she shook her head. "You don't understand, Ethan. I am a free spirit — a creature of the light."

143

He smiled a bit sadly. She tugged at his heart, and he truly wished he could tell her what she wanted to hear. But as it was, "I do understand Moira. But I also understand that each of our lives comes with its own burdens. Burdens we must learn to carry."

She stared at him momentarily, so long that he wondered if she understood what he said. And then she stood up, "It was good of you to come, Mr. Garraint. I will certainly consider what you have told me." And then she walked away, and he sighed deeply, taking one more sip of his coffee before he gathered his things and left.

03

As Ethan exited the library doors, a chill hit him that he had not expected. It had seemed that when he arrived, it would be a balmy autumn night, which was not so unusual for this part of the country. But something in the air had changed; something he had an instinctual feeling had nothing to do with the weather.

Slowly, he descended the granite steps, never letting his eyes leave the shadows that seemed unnaturally gathering in the parking lot. Once he reached level ground, he waited patiently for what exactly he had no idea. But something, every inch of his skin told him something was on its way.

Then finally, as if in direct answer to his anticipation, a figure stepped out of the darkness — a tall, lean man dressed rather immaculately in a grey suit with shoulder-length black hair.

He breathed a sigh of relief that would be tangible to no one but himself. It wasn't exactly that the new arrival was devoid of danger — just not particularly dangerous to him. After all, he was simply a bit player in this particular drama.

144

Being in no particular hurry, Ethan Garraint waited patiently for the man to approach, who, when doing so, paused just in front of him with a very slight smile crossing a particularly distinguished face.

"You might have given it a bit more time," Ethan directed toward this very old acquaintance, although in reality, the man physically didn't look a day over forty.

"There isn't time," he responded with a sereneness that Ethan always recalled seemed to be present in his manner.

Even in the very pale lamplight of the library steps, he could see the very dark blue eyes that he remembered his old friend possessing. Actually, it was the most animated aspect of his persona, those eyes which seemed to stretch deeply into infinity. That was if you were foolish enough to gaze too deeply within.

"Well, that's a pity, Nathaniel. She is confused and could use more time."

He nodded slowly, staring beyond him towards the library's front doors. "There is no choice. Even now, the others are planning their strike. If they succeed —" Then he stopped.

Ethan instinctively reached out and patted his friend's shoulder, instantly recognizing the chill he'd sensed in the air earlier. Of course, it had emanated from this ancient and powerful being. "Then let's make sure they don't."

The deep blue eyes focused on him again, and he felt compelled, even drawn to a place where his particular immortality had prevented him from ever finding — that place beyond in another sort of eternity that undeniably a part of him craved.

"Did you pave the way?"

He hesitated. Had he indeed done all he could have? Hard to say, not knowing what the outcome might be. "I did my best, Nathaniel. The rest is up to you." Then he stepped away from

145

him, donning the trench coat he'd been carrying across his arm, and headed toward the shadows before him. He did, however, pause for just an instant and call over his shoulder.

"Nathaniel, I have no actual evidence of this, but I do feel it. I believe she still loves you."

And then he continued to walk away, not particularly interested in waiting for a response because the dominant emotion he felt in the moment was envy.

&

Moira Archer's head began to swim. It was just thirty minutes until closing and then — and then. There was the rub. What would she do? Where would she go?

So much she had deliberately blocked from her mind so that she could do what she wanted. Her legs felt like lead as she walked, was compelled to go there — just take one more look to see if what Ethan Garraint had told her could possibly be true.

She moved beyond the information desk to right in front of the tall wall of glass where the fracture had occurred.

Her eyes slowly drifted into another state of seeing. Now it became more obvious. It was a glowing light, gathering, not outside, not inside, but within the cracks of the panes — glowing like some strange insects, fireflies perhaps but those which gave off a ruddy, irritated-looking, reddish-pink glow.

"You have the gift of sight Mneme," her mother had told her. "And the gift of healing and merging the light with the darkness. So many gifts, my child. Your life is one filled with destiny. You are the bridge." So young she'd been told this, and so young she'd been given away in an arranged marriage long ago. It had been frightening and then uncanny. It wasn't as if she were unhappy, just puzzled, curious as to what she did not have.

Her eyes were drawn back to the window. She could feel them, feel them near her skin, buzzing angrily, hungry, ravenous, in fact. She could feel them gathering strength, pushing against the cracks in the glass, determined to spread the opening further and further.

"Until they gain entrance to this world." The voice came from behind her and sent an instinctive shiver up her spine.

"To what end?" she murmured without looking back, although she felt him move beside her.

And then she began to feel that instinctual draw toward him — the one she had felt on her wedding day. She'd been so filled with terror learning she would be the bride of the master of death himself, but then she'd seen him, and all the fear had melted away. And there had been the pull, that magnetic pull that had been so nearly impossible to overcome.

"They feel the balance has been disrupted. It is their chance to enter and feed on humanity."

"Feed?" she whispered.

"In all kinds of ways. Energy to begin, then life itself, so there is no peace, no transition."

"I thought that was your domain."

She felt him sigh. He was weary. She could feel it within her as it had always been with them. "That's not really fair, is it, my dear? I do not take life. I am simply there to ensure transition once it is time."

She turned slowly to Nathaniel, feeling tears slipping down her cheeks. "I'm sorry. I'm not trying to hurt you."

"This goes beyond you and me," he stated softly. "But you could have come to me if you were so unhappy."

Her heart hurt like a tangible stab. How she'd missed him. How she had fought so hard not to acknowledge it. "I needed to be here, to remember living. To remember who I was. If I'd come to you."

"If," he repeated.

"I would not have had the strength to leave."

Slowly, he nodded in understanding, she thought; his dark eyes filled with so many emotions that she could easily allow herself to drown in them. "And did you? Did you find what you sought, my beloved?"

"Maybe. I think I'm still looking. I don't know, but it seems it's over."

And then he smiled softly. "All that is needed is the balance between us, death and memory. The balance must be restored. The discord must end."

"I don't understand," she said in confusion.

"If you wish to stay for a while, you can. If you only return at times, and of course, allow me to visit you."

She looked at him with surprise, a compromise, quite unexpected. "You mean something like six months of the year?"

His dark eyes sparkled. "Something like that if, of course, you agree to take me back as your husband."

She smiled, noting that the ugly fireflies at the broken window had begun to thin bit."

"I've missed you, my love," she whispered.

She felt Nathaniel softly take her hand in his. "We have much to talk of," he said as she gazed at her husband, feeling her heart begin to lighten.

"Yes, that is true."

The Lady in the Blue Dress

6 x 9 Softcover & Hardcover 214 pages
ISBN 978-1-61342-600-5
ISBN (Hardcover) 978-1-61342-418-6

When she was a child, Mika Devalieur was introduced to her grandmother's most precious possession — a priceless and mysterious painting that she simply called The Lady in the Blue Dress. Upon Adele St. Clair's death, the painting is left in the care of her granddaughter with only one stipulation. Mika must hand over the family heirloom to a total stranger. Mika Devalieur desperately wants to deny her beloved grandmother's last request, but she can't. Torn between her Gran's last wishes and her desire to hold onto the Lady, she ultimately journeys to rural Virginia, where an enigmatic man shows her that this painting is only the beginning.

What quickly becomes clear is that James Clairmont knows much more about her and the Lady than he is letting on. He begins to slowly unravel a powerful supernatural connection that spans three generations of her family. Mika finds herself desperate to uncover the entire truth before she falls in love with a man filled with so many secrets — secrets about him, about her, and most especially about The Lady in the Blue Dress. (First published on Kindle Vella, episodes 1-23.)

Dumaine Street
6 x 9 Softcover & Hardcover 306 pages
ISBN 978-1-61342-902-0
ISBN (Hardcover) 978-1-61342-416-2

Voices in her head, catastrophic emotions, hallucinations — Rebecca Wells is more than convinced that she is losing her mind. And as a last-ditch effort, she contacts a self-professed counselor who seems convinced he can help.

Gabriel Sutton has abandoned the world of medicine to navigate a realm filled with psychic phenomena. Diagnosing Becca with extreme empathic abilities, he struggles to help her stabilize her gifts while trying desperately not to fall in love with his patient.

From the realm of vulnerability into a crusade to use their profound gifts to rescue others from peril on the other side of death, these two follow an astonishing and unpredictable path into each other's hearts.

The Tethering
A Portent of Crows
6 x 9 Softcover & Hardcover 201 pages
ISBN 978-1-61342-599-2
ISBN (Hardcover) 978-1-61342-419-3

Deborah Brandt's beloved Aunt Gena always told her that she was special, a bit different, and would have to live her life, unlike other people. Of course, this she disregarded as the ramblings of her lovely but notably eccentric aunt. Although there were the things that Aunt Gena said that seemed true — like Deborah being sensitive to energy shifts, having potentially psychic impressions, and dreaming of a spirit guide — none of it could be real. But the most ridiculous thing that her Aunt Gena told her before she died was that someone special was out there for her. She said that he was an extraordinary man who was not only her perfect match but someone who she would learn from so that they could help the world in difficult times. How ridiculous! It sounds like a fairy tale, and no such person exists.

Daniel Wren is unique. He has been raised and trained from a young age to hone his psychic gifts. He lives in a world unimagined by most. And he has been waiting for years to contact his counterpart, soulmate, if you will. But the problem is that she is painfully unaware of the type of life that he lives and the life she would be entering into if they came together.

His dilemma becomes how best to proceed. How can he win her over and move forward before outside forces take that decision away from him?

Travels into the Breach
Accounts of a Reluctant Mystic
6 x 9 Softcover & Hardcover 171 pages
ISBN 978-1-61342-323-3
ISBN (Hardcover) 978-1-61342-417-9

At first glance, his life seems quiet, serene, and even uneventful. Malachi McKellan, a 65-year-old widower and author of esoteric books, lives largely as a recluse in a house situated just off the banks of Bayou St. John in New Orleans. But unbeknownst to most, he is also a bit of a detective, a specific kind of detective whose specialty is psychic attacks. Alongside his lifelong companion and spirit guide Simon Tull, a 19th-century, 20-something English gent, Malachi battles the unseen, and is an unacknowledged hero to the most vulnerable. Most of the population have no idea what is really happening beneath the surface of the world in which they live.

In this collection of adventures, Malachi McKellan and Simon Tull wage war against the most insidious elements of the paranormal. In *The Three*, Malachi and Simon come to the aid of a young woman being victimized by a group of dark witches. An old apartment building is the scene of an unimaginable battle against monstrous forces in *The Lost Soul*. Malachi and Simon find themselves strategizing against a psychic vampire in *Obsession*, and *The Hotel* turns back time to the 1980s where Malachi confronts a demonic spirit. In *Between*, a past life is revisited as Malachi attempts to rescue a beloved sister from committing her existence to vengeance, and *The Wedding* takes a personal turn when Malachi must confront painful truths while endeavoring to protect his niece from a potentially devastating union.

Travel into the breach with a pair of paranormal warriors who choose to confront overwhelming forces on a battlefield unsuspected by most.

Gravier's Bookshop
A New Orleans Paranormal Mystery (#1)
6 x 9 Softcover & Hardcover 172 pages
ISBN 978-1-61342-288-5
ISBN (Hardcover) 978-1-61342-411-7

Max Gravier had no intention of becoming a recluse, but after his wife's death it seems his life is heading in that direction. He spends his time running Gravier's Bookshop on Magazine Street and occasionally on the quiet helps the police solve a crime with his psychic sensitivities. That is until he answers Caroline Breslin's call, a cry for help out of his dreams that draws him into a fierce battle for a young woman's soul.

In this first installment of The New Orleans Paranormal Mystery series, Caroline Breslin, an amazingly gifted empath, is determined to strike out on her own and has moved out from the protection of her family home. All is going extremely well until, of course, she comes under siege from a devastating supernatural attack. The last thing Caroline wants is to run back to her family for help, even though she is painfully in over her head. What she really needs is a knight in shining armor — or maybe just that guy that keeps haunting her dreams.

Join them and the whole Breslin family psychic clan in this first installment of The New Orleans Paranormal Mystery Series where you'll travel into a new world just a few steps into the turbulent realm of the unseen.

The Hotel Mandolin
A New Orleans Paranormal Mystery (#2)
6 x 9 Softcover & Hardcover 146 pages
ISBN 978-1-61342-290-8
ISBN (Hardcover) 978-1-61342-412-4

Peril is wrapped up in the most enticing of disguises in *The Hotel Mandolin*, the second installment of The New Orleans Paranormal Mystery series. It's opulent, classic, and one of the most renowned hotels nestled deep in New Orleans' famous business district, but something is amiss at The Hotel Mandolin.

PI Peter Norfleet is calling out the big guns to help him investigate a recent suicide at the famous establishment — his good friend Max Gravier, a formidable psychic, and his girlfriend, Caroline Breslin, a talented empath. But none of them can seem to scratch the surface of this puzzle, no one except Cassie Breslin, Caroline's clairvoyant mother, who has somehow tapped into an unexpected connection with a tragic ghost from the turn of the century. And the more she uncovers, the more dangerous and malevolent the mystery becomes

The House at Pritchard Place
A New Orleans Paranormal Mystery (#3)
6 x 9 Softcover & Hardcover 138 pages
ISBN 978-1-61342-292-2
ISBN (Hardcover) 978-1-61342-413-1

Nothing is really wrong with the old Warrick House on Dante St. except that there most certainly is. Nothing is exactly wrong with its new mysterious owner except that Elise is sure that something doesn't add up. It isn't obvious, but sometimes the most dangerous things aren't.

In the third installment of The New Orleans Paranormal Mystery series, with the help of her very psychic sister and her children, the Breslin clan, Elise Ashford is about to embark on a wild rescue mission straight into another dimension that will land her squarely somewhere she doesn't expect, right back into her past. She'll land full circle; in a childhood home whose memory still haunts her to this day -- *The House at Pritchard Place.*

Treading on Borrowed Time
6 x 9 Softcover & Hardcover 223 pages
ISBN 978-1-61342-214-4
ISBN (Hardcover) 978-1-61342-436-0

For Julia Moreau, life seems complicated. Emerging from a failed marriage and managing a lifetime of diabetes, she lives alone in her childhood home where she communicates with the spirit of her Great Aunt Lilia. But Julia doesn't have a clue what complicated is until she is thrust into being the key chess piece in a match between two powerful men of extraordinary abilities on the wild hunt for a mystical creature hidden in the heart of New

Orleans' French Quarter. Will Julia lose her soul to the karma of a devastating past life or her heart to the love of a man driven by dark forces? What is clear is that whichever way she turns she is *Treading on Borrowed Time.*

Sanctuary of Echoes
6 x 9 Softcover & Hardcover 371 pages
ISBN 978-1-61342-211-3
ISBN (Hardcover) 978-1-61342-409-4

Ghosts unacknowledged do not sleep.

Corey Knight has resigned herself to a quiet, reclusive life spent living out the rest of her days in her childhood home on the fringes of New Orleans' French Quarter. But the unexpected specter of her deceased father plunges her into a mad quest for a missing supernatural weapon unearthed long ago. And unfortunately, her only ally is a lost love she once betrayed.

Iain Shaw returns to New Orleans, a city he abandoned a decade before while fleeing a devastating past. Here, he is forced to confront it again in the visage of the woman he once adored - one that he is now determined to get back at any cost.

Follow them both in a wild paranormal tale of discovery and redemption as they confront and unearth the echoes of a buried and unyielding truth that once tore them irreparably apart.

A Quiet Moment

6 x 9 Softcover & Hardcover 273 pages
ISBN 978-1-61342-326-4
ISBN (Hardcover) 978-1-61342-435-3

Jacob Wyss is caught in a rut, in fact on the verge of being engulfed by it. After an excruciating and disillusioning divorce, his life as an artist in a sleepy-college town at the foot of the Appalachian Mountains has become quiet, routine, and maddening in its predictability. One wintry day, his deep restlessness drives him out in precarious conditions to a largely empty bookstore nearly devoid of another living soul, nearly.

Aimee Marston isn't like everyone else. On the surface, she lives a sedate life working as a feature writer for a small local newspaper in addition to several other editorial jobs to help make ends meet. But just beneath, her existence is largely not her own. She is a sensitive, an empathetic psychic, guided by her calling to use her gifts to help others. Unfortunately, as a result, her secretiveness has made her defensive, protective of herself, and prevented her from having much of a life.

A psychic call for help sends Aimee out on a freezing January morning where her destiny and Jacob's collide sending both their lives spiraling onto an unexpected and often disturbing track. Two lonely souls connect, not by accident, but by design. Theirs is the intersection of two spiritual paths, two lovers who must struggle to overcome the phantoms of a past life, as well as the challenges of their own inner demons to carve out an extraordinary future together.

A Ghost of a Chance
6 x 9 Softcover & Hardcover 230 pages
ISBN 978-1-61342-162-8
ISBN (Hardcover) 978-1-61342-440-7

You never know what's coming next.

Jack Brennan, an ambitious high-powered attorney, dies. But that's not the end, rather only the beginning. He finds himself constrained to an inexplicable afterlife as an earth-bound spirit trapped in an old Virginia farmhouse. His only companion is a very much living, reclusive writer of campy vampire novels. The maddening problem is that Hallie does not know he is there, nor that he is somewhat reluctantly falling in love with her.

Hallie Barkly is recovering from a painful and disillusion-ing divorce. Out of the ashes of her former life, she has managed to somehow forge a career and exorcise her demons by writing under the pseudonym of Sebastian Winters. Slowly, she is awakening to the fact that she is not alone.

Their lives intersect, and two unconventional lovers are brought together under insurmountable circumstances. To-gether they must battle an unseen force hell-bent on possessing Hallie's life and bridge death itself to make possible what cannot be — to find a chance.

Dragonflies - Journeys into the Paranormal
6 x 9 Softcover & Hardcover 176 pages
ISBN 978-1-88756-072-6
ISBN (Hardcover) 979-8-32548-418-6

In every form of creation, there is a blueprint for living, for experience, for interpretation. In flight, they can twist, turn, alter direction, pause in midair, and even fly backward. The dragonfly is the master of adaptability. They are a living prism, refracting light, and color, seemingly shifting their essence.

The lesson the dragonfly gives is that life is never what it appears to be.

In "The Wizard," as a novice practitioner of magic, Aurora Finn finds herself battling against the illusions of a powerful wizard intent on separating her from the world she knows. "The Sojourners" is a gentle story of a mother and daughter whose tenancy in an old Virginia farmhouse uncovers the trials and sorrows of its former occupants. A bookstore clerk gets an extraordinary customer on Halloween night in "Late One Night at Berstrums Books." In "The Tear," a woman coping with her fatal illness unknowingly begins a track on a mystical journey that will entirely restructure her vision of the world.

These stories follow the path of the dragonfly imbued with the momentum and energy of change, taking a winding and treacherous journey that ultimately leads to truth buried beneath perception.

Breaking Through the Pale
6 x 9 Softcover 134 pages
ISBN 978-1-88756-045-0

Journey with metaphysical author Evelyn Klebert into a collection of short stories that travel beyond the pale into the unpredictable realm of the paranormal.

In "A Grey Mourning," a disillusioned man encounters a mysterious being on the foggy streets of New Orleans. "Contact" is a tale of automatic writing, when a young artist establishes communication with a spirit guide, and the victim of a car crash unravels the true nature of her existence in "Dancing on the Threshold." The final tale is called "Isolation," in which a con-fused and disoriented woman finds herself in an old, quaint house where she must piece together the mystical implications surrounding her predicament.

Explanations
6 x 9 Softcover 82 pages
ISBN 978-1-93493-515-6

In this, her second poetry collection, Evelyn Klebert takes us down the intricate path of a personal journey. Life with its particular struggles, pitfalls, and ultimately triumphs clearly begins to mirror a universal path, the quest for answers that we all ultimately pursue. In this reflective, esoteric collection we can all explore and seek some of life's elemental mysteries and hopefully when all is said and done emerge with some *Explanations*.

The Witches' Own

6 x 9 Softcover & Hardcover 140 pages
ISBN 978-1-61342-058-4
ISBN (Hardcover) 978-1-61342-428-5

On the surface things seem quiet and serene in the picturesque coastal village of Kilmarnock, Virginia. But something unseen roams its lush forests as the past and present collide and the unthinkable begins to wreak its vengeance. Young Lucy Bonner is executed for witchcraft in the town's distant and brutal past. Her death triggers an unholy chain of events which grasp at the restless heart of novelist Peter McQuade, spurring him towards a quest to uncover the dark and terrifying truth.

The Left Palm

And Other Halloween Tales of the Supernatural

6 x 9 Softcover & Hardcover 122 pages
ISBN 978-1-93493-556-9
ISBN (Hardcover) 978-1-61342-442-1

Halloween is the time of year when that veil between worlds is thinned, and you can just catch a quick glimpse into the realm of the unknowable. In this collection of short stories, Evelyn Klebert takes you to a place where ordinary life splinters into the sphere of the paranormal.

The journey begins with one woman's unstoppable quest for vengeance against a supernatural creature in "Wolves" and continues in an old historical graveyard where a horrifying discovery is uncovered in "Emma Fallon." In "The Soul Shredder," a psychiatrist's unusual patient opens his eyes to a disturbing new view of reality, while in "Wildflowers," a woman strikes up a supernatural friendship with impossible implications. And in "The Left Palm," a fortuneteller in the French Quarter receives a most unexpected and terrifying customer.

White Harbor Road
And Other Tales of Paranormal Romance
6 x 9 Softcover & Hardcover 152 pages
ISBN 978-1-61342-066-9
ISBN (Hardcover) 978-1-61342-441-4

A psychic soul mate, a time traveler, a horror writer, and an enigmatic stranger take a selection of resilient, life-battered heroines to a place of paranormal healing and transformation. In this collection of short stories, *White Harbor Road* is the last stop where life's burdens and hardships evolve into something unexpected.

Considerations
6 x 9 Softcover 84 pages
ISBN 978-1-88756-062-7

Sometimes the struggle to understand the meaning and complexities of living comes down to a single moment of introspection or a fleeting yet meaningful reflection. This collection of poetry by Evelyn Klebert takes you down a winding path of self-discovery where the resolution may not always be absolute, but the journey is indeed unforgettable. It a wide and varied map of inspired poetry for your examination and consideration.

Appointment with the Unknown
The Hotel Stories
6 x 9 Softcover & Hardcover 155 pages
ISBN 978-1-61342-360-8
ISBN (Hardcover) 978-1-61342-421-6

A hotel, for most, represents a normal place, a predictable realm of commonality. One might even go as far to say a safe space, the reliable where nothing particularly unusual is expected to happen. Or is it? Dimensional traveling, spirit guides, mystical storms, and soul mates separated by time are only a few elements dotting this supernatural landscape. Drop into a collection of romantic paranormal stories where that place of commonality is only the threshold, the jumping-off point, for extraordinary adventures into the unknown.

Visit Evelyn's website at:
www.evelynklebert.com

Cornerstone Book Publishers
www.cornerstonepublishers.com